THE GOLDEN IMAGE

13 Stories from the Citizens of Sheridan Falls

By

R.R. LaVaughn

LaVaughn

Printed in the United States of America

All characters and events are fiction. Any resemblance to real people or incidents is purely coincidental.

Published by LaVauri Publishing House
www.lavauri.com

For more information on this book
https://www.lavauri.com/thegoldenimage.html

Look for these books by R.R. LaVaughn

Fiction:
Repeat Offender
When Roses Cry

Look for these books by Ricky LaVaughn

Non-Fiction:
Foundation of the Fire
In The Beginning

ISBN: 978-0615671192

ACKNOWLEDGEMENTS

I have to thank God for blessing me with this opportunity and idea. To all my family and friends, you are great and your support keeps me going. In addition, I want to thank everyone who has bought my books in the past and told others to do the same.

TABLE OF CONTENTS

PRIME POSITION

2 Kings 22

Sheridan Falls, home to at least 100,000 people and a tourist getaway. It has two main attractions that bring in thousands of people each year. We have pristine beaches that are white and the sand is very smooth. There are shells that have been finely grinded with the sand and reflect the sun giving the beach a radiant look.

The biggest beach, Glasgow Beach and Park, is actually a resort area. Several hotels and resorts dot the landscape on the two-mile long ocean front property. In spite of the hotels area, there are plenty of public spaces for visitors. Many come to surf, scuba dive, motor boat, play water sports, swim, and horseback through the water. There was talk to allow a cruise line to buy a piece of the beach so they could dock in summer and spring. The city council denied this but things could change in the future.

There are some parts of the Sheridan Falls coastline where tourists won't go. Companies use those areas for shipping and delivery. Sheridan Falls handle a variety of seafood and electronics trade for U.S. companies delivering goods to the region.

The other tourist attraction is the falls in the highland areas of the city. It's technically within city limits but still far away. There's one main waterfall where the city derives a part of its name. It's roughly a seventy-seven foot tall single drop waterfall. The city engineers where able to build a walkway to go around this fall so people could get within ten feet of the falling water. Tourists love to get that close to the falls and reach out to touch nature's falling stream. The engineers where smart and put up strong guardrails so no one would fall over while attempting this stunt. Many residents, like me, take the waterfalls for granted. It's beautiful but I still prefer the beaches.

I have other things on my mind. It's the start of my last year in high school, and I'm thrilled. Last school season my classmates voted me senior class president. That is an honor, but what energizes me is the desire to do something great. Already I have completed some college classes and plan on taking more. Architecture is tough, so it's a good idea to get a head start on the basic courses. I'm glad Sheridan State offer classes at both city high schools.

I'm proud at being a student of Brent High's senior class. There where opportunities to go to a private school but that's not my style. My friends are here, I can take college courses, good-looking girls, and they voted me class president. Takashi Kaneko, class president does sound nice, and looks great on college applications.

"Takashi," someone yells. I snap out of my daydream and look around the basketball court. "You still playing," Donn asks.

Its lunchtime and playing basketball is a good way to start the school year. Donn is a member of the senior council as well. He's the class treasure and avid basketball player. Like me, he wants to use the council as filler for his college application. He's good at basketball, but not so great that he can get any scholarship he wants. Doing other things will show that he's balanced, intelligent, and athletic.

"Yeah," I respond. Donn bounces me the ball and gets into position for the three-on-three game. Donn, with another guy on the cabinet, as well as me is going against my best friend, Seth and a couple juniors. Seth and I have known each other for years. Even before, we came to Brent together.

Seth guards me as soon as I dribble the ball. It's great playing against your friend even though he's a better player and knows it. I can shoot the three so at least I'm not worthless. Plus, I have Donn on my team. All I have to do is get him the ball and get out the way.

Our teams play for a while. It's back and forth but Donn is clearly helping our senior cabinet threesome. I knock in a long-range shot from time to time, but Donn's athletic moves are no match for Seth and his teammates. We take a break with our team up by five. The lunch period is going to end in 15 minutes and we get some water to cool down. During our break, a girl strolls up in our direction covered in mud.

The six of us keep talking assuming she's going to walk by and go inside the school. I've seen her before in one of the special classes for people who have various learning disabilities. Our school and Wedgewood, the other high school, have classrooms for them. Years ago, they use to put everyone with special learning in one of the old elementary schools. People complained, so they split the group and put them between the two high schools.

Donn is in the middle of talking about a high score he got on a war game he was playing when the girl walks right up to our group. She looks right at me, caked in mud. It covered her hair, clothes, and shoes. Various cuts littered her face, and bruises were on parts of her arms. There is silence, but she ends the break.

"Hi, my name is Claudeen," she says. "Do I meet your satisfaction?"

"Excuse me," I respond. Some of the guys chuckle so I assume this is a joke.

"Do I meet your satisfaction," she asks louder. Her movements is jerky and she stares into my eyes pleading for what I assume was acceptance.

"I heard you Claudeen," I respond. "But why are you covered in mud? Why would that satisfy me?"

"I don't want to hurt anymore," Claudeen starts, "I'm tired of being embarrassed and punched."

"Go on now," Donn orders. "Takashi doesn't have time for this."

"Wait Donn," I say. Claudeen shifts her attention from Donn to me. I can see the fear in her eyes and looks at me for help. "I don't know you," I begin, "why would I hurt you?"

"Every cabinet does it," Claudeen responds.

"Say, what," I ask.

Ms. Hampton come over and walks up to Claudeen. "Let's get you cleaned up," Ms. Hampton says. Claudeen looks into the teacher's eyes and follows. She turns her head and stares at me. I don't know what to do, but she is seeking a resolution. I give her the thumbs up. She smiles and follows Ms. Hampton with ease.

"What was that about," Seth asks.

"I don't know," I say. I have some suspicions on some rumors that some of the students bullied the slower classes. No one openly complained and for the most part they where just rumors. It was nothing like the situations I heard over at Wedgewood. Apparently, they have a small gang problem. I'm glad we aren't like them.

Seth and I talk about the situation after the lunch break. We knew it had to be bad for Claudeen to show up covered in mud and self mutilated. I didn't know what had went on, but it had to of been horrible. I'm glad Ms. Hampton came over. She's a young teacher, but very wise. The humorous thing is how many of my fellow seniors try to ask her to the homecoming dance in six weeks. They assume that because they where 18, dating a teacher was legal. They couldn't be further from the truth, but I can't blame them for trying.

After school, Seth and I look up some information on the bullying. We want to see if anyone wrote about abuses or bullying special needs students. There is small stuff but nothing concrete. We even try talking to people on Twitter, Facebook, and various other sites. Nothing came up. Finally, it hit me. I am going to have to go to the source that brought this to my attention. Claudeen.

The next day at school, I make it a point to meet with Claudeen. While in homeroom, I realize that I don't know her schedule and assume that it will not line up with mine. This will make it hard to meet up with her by chance in the hallways or study hall. Because of this, I decide to meet with her during lunch. At least I know that we have that in common.

Claudeen is with some of her classmates near the edge of the soccer field. Donn and Seth wants me to play basketball but I decline after telling them what I plan on doing. Seth joins me and we walk towards Claudeen.

Being class president is serious. I couldn't stand myself if I at least didn't learn what was going on and how to help others within my power. Claudeen sees me walk in her direction. A few of her friends run off, but the others stay at her behest. She gives them the thumbs up like I gave, assuring them that I wasn't going to hurt anybody. Some of the guys look cautious which is funny because they are all bigger then me. Maybe they think that because I represent the cabinet, trouble is sure to come.

"Claudeen," I call out. She smiles, with a half crook in her face and skip towards me.

"You gave the thumbs up," she says. "You were satisfied?"

"Yes," I respond. "Very much so."

Many of her friends smile and giggle. They are happy at my response. I guess Claudeen served as a sacrificial lamb for the group so no one else would get injured or embarrassed. She has a few scratches on her face and I'm sure the bruises will heal. It's impressive that she did this for her classmates.

"I have some questions, you don't mind do you," I ask.

Claudeen looks at her friends then at me. "No," she responds hesitantly. Many of them start to leave but I put my hands up.

"You don't have to go," I say. Then I return my attention to Claudeen. "You're safe."

She smiles and says, "Okay, what's your question."

"How long has this been going on?"

"Since the beginning," Claudeen responds.

"When you got here," Seth asks. The group turn their attention to him and then at me. His voice is ripe with anger that frightens some of them. Seth probably seems like he was mad at them, but in reality his rage was against whomever started this mess.

"No, I'm a junior. It was here way before me."

"You said the cabinet, have they done this?"

Claudeen is nervous. Her fingers fidget as she looks around for comfort. I can hear her gulp. "It's safe," Claudeen asks.

"Yes."

Claudeen pause and blows out a long sigh. "Yes," she responds. "Each year, the senior leaders secretly embarrass and hurt us."

That hit my heart like a stone in water. It wasn't just regular students being bullies but the leaders of the school. They where never suppose to hurt classmates. Here I am judging Wedgewood and my own school has a bullying problem.

"How long," I ask. Then it dawns on me, I technically already asked that question.

"Since the beginning," she answers.

"Beginning?" It hits me. This started once they integrated the schools with the special education students. "Why?"

"Enunciation, I think."

"Initiation," I help. Claudeen nods.

"Each year, we earn our right to be here."

"I'm sorry," I say while massaging my temples. Seth shakes his head in disbelief. No one has the right to do this.

"You don't have to be sorry," Claudeen says with a smile, "You accepted my humiliation."

"You shouldn't have to do that," I respond. "As long as I can help it, this will stop."

The school bell rung. Seth and I walk to the doors while Claudeen and classmates ran to the building. They probably feel better but I am a mess. The thought that they have to earn their way into being a student at Brent was ludicrous. I wasn't sure if the president of the senior class initiates this behavior but it was going to stop with me.

The next day Donn wants to speak with me at lunch. I assume it was about some of the issues on the senior cabinet. We didn't have much in plans, but our biggest issue is the Homecoming dance. We worked on the matter during the summer with the other cabinet members. Donn, being the treasure, knew how much money we had to help the school. He has ideas for fundraisers we can do to raise more.

We meet on the side of the school leaning against the wall. A few freshman girls walk by and wave. We do our custom head nod and then waited for them to leave.

"Heard you spoke with the retarded girl," Donn says.

"Claudeen," I correct. "And you shouldn't call her retarded."

"I know, I'm just playing," he says.

"She told me some stuff. Crazy, unbelievable stuff."

Donn says, "I'm sure she stretched the truth a little, everyone does."

I pause for a moment and stare at Donn. This isn't a shock to him. I'm not sure what he knows but his behavior seems like its okay to abuse others.

"Donn, I don't think you know what's going on. She said previous senior classes privately embarrassed and hurt them so they could earn their way into school."

"Yeah," Donn responds. His response is flat. He knows. It's not a shock to him.

"That's all you can say. Yeah. Did you know about this?"

"You didn't," Donn responds.

"No," I answer. I shake my head and am speechless. The words are trying to come out to convince him that hurting others is wrong. You can't treat people like this. This is a school not a private organization.

"You can't stop this. I already have ideas," Donn says.

"Don't care," I respond.

"Excuse me?"

"I don't care what your ideas are," I say. "It ends with us."

Donn is visibly upset. He crosses his arms and nostrils flare open. He's trying to intimidate me with his size and muscular body. He knows I can't fight. That doesn't matter. The behavior of treating any student at Brent as second-class citizens is going to end with me.

"You're spitting in the face of tradition. We didn't start it Takashi, but it's in our best interest to continue."

"I vomit in the face of tradition. It ends with us Donn. Period."

Donn can see that he is not going to change my mind. He walks away and head towards the courts. I don't want to see him out on the courts and walk inside the school. My mind is in shock at his blatant disregard for others people's well-being.

Throughout the rest of the week, I spoke with some people, trusted friends, on the subject. Most of them had never heard about mistreating some of our classmates. Then again, none of them is close to the mentally or physically challenged. They like me were surprised.

Many of my friends gave various and good suggestions. Mona Wilkerson told me to continue standing up for them. She didn't know that it was going on, but that a strong leader should stare adversity in the face and overcome that situation. Marcy, one of the relatives from the founder of Sheridan Falls, told me to do what was right. "Tradition is stupid," she said. I knew she would say that. She has a nerdy-goth mix to her style. Seth heard Claudeen's statement and was on my side.

At the end of the week, the senior cabinet has a brief meeting. It was made of me, the VP, secretary, treasure, plus a few council members. In total, we have seven. Donn and I never joke during the meeting causing everyone to feel uncomfortable. They know our friendship so the others can tell something is wrong.

After the meeting, one of the council members, Jason Templeton, wants to talk. We go a few doors down from the room near the physics class.

"Have a minute," Jason asks.

"Quick one."

"What's the matter?"

Jason is another one of the family members from the founding families of Sheridan Falls. The Templetons don't get as much credit as the Sheridans but they where here together. Of course, this was more then two hundred years ago, so it's not as if it was his grandfather or something. I do know Jason and Marcy are close friends. Not sure if it's more then that.

"Do you know," I ask him.

"Know what?"

"That the mentally challenged students are being abused."

Jason squints and cocks his head to the side. He doesn't know. "What," he asks.

I explain to him what Claudeen said to me. Most of the dialogue is in whispers. Can't let other people hear our conversation. Jason is surprised to hear that Donn and other cabinet members knew about the abuse.

"Speak with Ms. Hampton," Jason suggests. "She's our advisor."

I agree and meet with Ms. Hampton after school. It's Friday so she doesn't mind making a little time. I drive to school, staying a little longer isn't a problem. We meet in her overly decorated and full of color classroom.

"Something on your mind Takashi," Ms. Hampton asks. Her voice is high and almost piercing. It's probably why new seniors assume she is close to our age.

"Yes," I respond. From there I tell her some of the troubling information I learned. Unlike with Jason, I didn't give her names of people who I believed would want to continue the tradition. Although that could help the situation, I never thought it was good to be a tattletale.

Ms. Hampton thought about my dilemma and sighs. She's thinking about her advice. I'm sure when I walk in she assumes the issue would be on the homecoming dance or planting daises by the trees.

"It's interesting," Ms. Hampton starts.

"What is?"

"That us and Wedgewood is going through a similar but different situation."

"They're bullying situation is out of control," I respond.

"And this isn't?"

I thought about what she said and nod. "Touché."

"What's really weird is that at Wedgewood some young guy is stirring up a little trouble and asking about the bullies. He wants to put an end to the problem."

"How do you know this?"

"Teacher stuff," Ms. Hampton responds. "We talk. The thing about it is that you're in a similar but even more complicated situation. This is because people don't know we have a problem. How do you punish an invisible problem?"

"Thanks Ms. Hampton," I say.

"That's it? You don't want to hear my idea. I have an analogy on being an adventurer and taking chances that can help."

"Maybe later," I respond. "But you gave me a good idea."

That weekend I talk with Seth. We hash out a plan that will help Claudeen and her friends. Ms. Hampton is right. We have to reveal to people what is going on without being tattletales. Unlike Wedgewood where everyone knows about the bullying situation, we have to reveal that there's a problem. The best place to do this is at Homecoming.

I wait for the moment when Claudeen is with her classmates in the cafeteria. It's raining and most of the peoples stay inside to eat and play card games. Rumors spread on how Wedgewood ended their bullying situation. It wasn't a secret so it was easier for them to deal with the problem directly. The young guy pulled it off and was able to help his school. Now it's my turn.

At the lunch table, I talk with my friends and move to various tables in the cafeteria. I do this on purpose to show everyone that all people are equal. We're all Brent High Unicorns and none of us is better or worst then any other.

Finally, the time came for me to start the plan.

"Hey Claudeen," I say.

"Hello," she responds.

"Got a date for Homecoming?"

"No, I never do," she says. She shrugs her shoulders and plays with her long hair. "But it's okay…"

"Wanna' be mine?"

There is silence at the table and the ones next to us. Many people hear my request but can't believe it. Why would the senior class president ask someone from the special education class to homecoming? There are plenty of girls interested in me. Maybe not plenty but quite a few, I think.

"You're joking," she asks.

"No, no I'm not."

"Uh…"

"How about I give you some time," I suggest.

"No, I mean yes. I mean no you don't have to give me time, but yes, I would go."

I smile, thank her, and tell her that I have some business to attend. She is happy and talks with her friends.

To most people I was insane but Seth knows the plan. We had an idea and hope it will help. Claudeen has already been a physical sacrificial lamb for her friends but after homecoming, she'll never have to self-humiliate while at Brent.

The days in between asking Claudeen to the Homecoming dance, many people ask what I was thinking. I told them she was sweet and cute. Claudeen would sometimes have a blank look with her eyes wide open and a crooked grin. Her face structure is perfectly even on both sides and the hair flows well past the middle of her back. Besides, I wanted to hang out with her.

In the hall after chemistry, Donn pulls me to the side. We didn't speak much since the argument on the side of the school. Both of us have study hall at the same time and walk in that direction.

"What are you doing," Donn ask.

"Going to study hall, like you."

"Not that. You and Claudeen?"

"We're not a couple, just going to homecoming together."

We keep walking but at a slower pace so the conversation wouldn't be in study hall.

"You think this is going to save her or those kids in the special-ed class," Donn says with his voice full of hate.

"If you spent time with them, you wouldn't see them like that."

"If you think, that going on a date with her will protect them, you're wrong. Greg likes the plans I got. You can't stop us."

Greg is the Vice-President of the senior class. I knew he had something to do with the situation. He's probably the main leader with Donn helping him. We stop in front of the study hall room. I stare at the door and then down the hall. A little ways and to the left are the special education classes for the junior and seniors.

"Yes I will. And I will do everything I can, to put an end to you, Greg, and anyone else who abuses their power."

We didn't have anything to say after that. We went into the class our separate ways. Donn disappoints me. I can't believe he feels like it's his right to hurt others.

Homecoming takes place in the school gym. The entire room is full of gold and white, the school colors. We where happy because our football team won the night before which brought more excitement to the dance.

The king and queen of the dance are the starting Quarterback and Head Cheerleader. No shock, no surprises. Sometimes, you get the most random of people to win but not now. That was fine and didn't care about that. My goal was to expose the senior cabinet for trying to hurt their own classmates.

During the dance, I have a feeling that the members of the group will come after Claudeen. She already tossed mud on herself at the beginning of the school year. To the student body it wouldn't be a surprise if she were caught doing something else that was strange. No one would suspect someone from the cabinet to be a part.

Claudeen tells me she has to use the restroom after a Spandau Ballet's hit song ends. I'm cool with that and look at Seth. We knew that we have to follow her because the cabinet might make their move. One part of the plan was for me to follow from a distance so their plan can start but she wouldn't get hurt. I didn't want them to stop what they where doing so Seth and I can catch them in the act.

When Claudeen left, I wait for a few seconds and leave after but the secretary of the senior cabinet, Joy, stops me. She wants a dance but I refuse. She is persistent and I can tell something is wrong. I lead Joy to the dance floor and spin her quickly. She smiles and then stops to see that I'm already heading off the dance floor and into the hallway.

Claudeen is down the hall and turns the corner when a few members of the cabinet follow her. I don't see Seth but assume that he is in position as well. Joy might follow me, so I decide to take a different route and go upstairs. After that, I make my way down the hall and walk down the stairs where I know Claudeen will be.

Claudeen steps out the restroom to see Donn, Greg, and a few members of the senior cabinet. She recognizes them and hunches her shoulders.

"Takashi said that it was done. That I had fulfilled my commitment," Claudeen nervously says.

"No," Donn responds. "That was self-inflicted. It can't be like that."

"Besides," Greg starts, "You now have to be an example to Takashi for going against us."

"I don't want to be hurt. Please don't," Claudeen pleas.

"Get the urine," Greg calls over to one of the cabinet members. "Soak her down and punch her ribs. They already think she's crazy for the mud stunt and scratching herself."

"Leave her alone," I command.

I heard some of what they said and ran down the hall. They plan on embarrassing Claudeen by splashing her with urine. Disgusting. I can't believe they all brought their own to splash Claudeen. That's awful. Then to punch her in the ribs, that's criminal.

"Takashi," Donn starts, "this Captain American stunt has gone on long enough. Grab a bottle and show yourself to be the leader that you are."

"I am," I respond. I stand in front of Claudeen to protect her from liquid human waste.

"It's tradition," Joy says.

"One that should be broken."

"Since this school start letting misfits in, every senior class has put them in their place," Greg says.

"I made a promise to Claudeen and her classmates. This stops with us."

"You leave us no choice but to include you with this," Donn says and wave his free hand in Claudeen's direction. He is furious and has a bottle of urine ready to go.

"So be it," I respond.

Right before Donn was going to squeeze, there is a sound of heels coming down the hall. "Stop right there," a high-pitched voice says. Ms. Hampton is running down the hall. Seth comes from around the corner holding a camera. He taped the entire conversation and had time to tell Ms. Hampton. It was perfect. The group admitted to past issues and their plans to harm current students.

"Put the bottles down now," Ms. Hampton orders. When she is authoritative, some of that squeakiness goes away.

The same issue, bullying, stops at Brent High as it did in Wedgwood. The methods are different but both are effective. The administrators replace most of the senior class cabinet due to their actions on tape at trying to harm Claudeen and myself. Many of the senior class leadership, who where not on tape, got their positions elevated, like Jason.

What's great is that people at school didn't see me as a nark. My classmates respect me for standing up to people and revealing a secret that has permeated the school for decades. Of course, previous senior classes denied their involvement of such actions but the students they affected say otherwise.

A few days after homecoming, I'm able to speak with Claudeen alone during lunch. There is a nagging feeling that I have done something wrong while trying to do something right. I have to apologize.

"Sorry Claudeen for using you," I say.

"You didn't use me," she responds. Claudeen doesn't see how I used her as a part of my plan to help the special education youth. I knew that by asking her out, Claudeen would make a perfect target and easier for me to reveal the cabinet's true purpose. It worked, but had I been late Claudeen would be soaked in urine and her ribs bruised.

"Yeah, I did," I say. I explain to her what happened as well as Seth and mine plan. The truth is I did like spending time with her as a friend. She's a great person who has a wonderful heart but I'm not trying to be romantically involved. After I said my spill, she responds.

"You saved me," she says. "I don't care how it happened, but you got it done."

"True."

"You where willing to take urine for me. No one has been willing to take the beating or embarrassment that others had for me. No one."

"I was in prime position to help. I couldn't let that happened," I say.

Claudeen hugs me and smile. "Thank you." I hug her back and a little tear streams out of my eye.

Don't be afraid to break tradition, especially if it helps others in their situation and build a relationship with God.

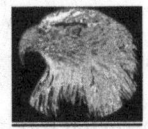

IN MY HANDS

Matthew 14:13-21

Its black Friday, as many people call the day after Thanksgiving, but I don't participate. I'm ready for Christmas, so going out at night in the midst of a rabid crowd is not my idea of fun. Instead, my daughter wants to go and get some gifts for my grandchildren. Because she desires to surprise them, I agree to watch and spend some time with the two little ones. Besides, I need the help hanging the Christmas decoration.

I decide to change the décor a little and go with a different color scheme. For the past several years, I've decorated with Green and Gold bulbs and white lights. That was Henry's favorite so I obliged. Henry is my husband. I should say former husband. We had his homegoing at least three years ago. The yearly tribute of lights to him was nice but it's time to move on.

Talking with my daughter and two granddaughters, I decide to go with Silver, Cobalt, and Ice Blue. It doesn't seem very Christmas like but they enjoyed picking out the ornaments and LED lights. They're unique and brighter then what I'm used too. Especially the cobalt blue lights that are almost hurting my eyes.

"Grandma, should we start on the banister," Penny the youngest between the two girls ask. It sounds strange having Grandma as my title. I should've gotten them to call me Mimi, G-maw, or something else. Oh well. I smile and look her way.

"That's a great idea Penny. Then we can eat some of Marsha's cookies before completing the tree."

"Sounds good to me," Marsha calls from the kitchen. She's a unique blend. Marsha loves sports and is the leader on her middle school basketball team. A few of the girls from the previous year left so now she's the star. She loves to mirror her game after a local standout, Mona Wilkerson. She's well known and already has a scholarship. The thing I like about her is that I hear Mona is studious and cares for people. I keep telling Marsha to mimic those behaviors as well as the basketball. Marsha also loves baking, cooking, and sewing her own skirts. She's tomboyish and prissy at the same time.

Marsha walks into the living room wearing an old Jordan shirt and jeans. A cooking smock is around her with powdered sugar crumbs on the front.

"I'm trying out some new recipes," Marsha says.

"That's cool," Penny responds.

"You know we love your cookies," I say.

"Good, I can also make some deli sandwiches as well. Once we're finished eating I'll come in and help with the tree." I nod and she walks back into the kitchen almost skipping with joy.

While putting the lights around the family room banister, Penny pauses for a moment and looks at me. She's eight but very inquisitive. Her older sister, Marsha, tends to go with life as it comes. It's probably what makes her a great basketball player.

"What's the matter Penny," I ask her.

"Nothing," Penny responds. I know she's thinking of something and smile at her. "Well," she begins. "Marsha and I were talking about our favorite moments on different holidays." Now that's an interesting conversation. Then again, these two tend to do that. Most girls talk about their favorite shows, hairstyles, or dolls. Marsha and Penny discuss, school politics, characters in the Bible, and apparently holidays.

"Okay," I respond.

"And after we talked a bit I couldn't think of a favorite moment on Thanksgiving."

"You can't?"

"No," Penny says. "It's just overeating."

"Overeating," I say. "Thanksgiving is more then that."

Penny stops hanging the lights and look at me. One eyebrow up and her arms folded. "You mean the Indians and Pilgrims?"

"No, not just them." I stop hanging the lights as well and walk to the couch. Various icicle ornaments and sparkling silver balls are in their boxes on the chair and floor waiting to be used on the eight-foot tall tree in the front room. I pat the cushion next to me for Penny to sit down. "Let me tell you my favorite memory of Thanksgiving."

Penny sits down and with great anticipation says, "Okay."

LaVaughn

****

Many years ago, when I was your age, my mother ran a non-profit center helping the homeless. Connected to the center was a food pantry to help those who had a home but needed food. She made sure to keep the two separate, realizing that both groups needed different things. Because she ran a food pantry and homeless shelter, Thanksgiving and Christmas was her busiest time of year. She always made sure to be prepared for the holidays, but a recession cut into the normal giving from the community.

When times are tough it's hard thinking of others when you barely have the means to provide for yourself. Family has to come first and most people held true to that rule. People and companies giving from their surplus of food and money provided mom's supply. Some companies helped but many pantries and shelters in the city where in need as well.

A week before Thanksgiving, Mom talked with the family. She tried to relax but her mind kept drifting to the lack of food problem at the shelter. Dad tried to comfort and let her know that things will be okay, Mom wasn't having it.

"I can help," I told mom. I remembered the story a week earlier at church about the young boy who brought some fish and bread for lunch. Jesus used that small portion of food and was able to feed thousands of people.

She patted me on the head and said, "Sure you can Myra." At the time that made me feel good, but I realized later that she was patronizing me. She didn't believe that I could help.

Mom meant to pacify me but it ended fueling my desire to give. I hadn't hit double digit in age, but was determined to help my mother. I knew how important her job was, and figured that helping her would help those people. The homeless and hungry were strangers to me but that didn't matter. My own dinner table was fine with the food provided by my parents and hunger never crossed my mind. I couldn't imagine that during a time of Thanksgiving, others might have to go without.

The next day I talked with my classmates about the situation. At the time, the only thing they knew is how much they loved to eat and couldn't imagine others not doing the same. They said they would ask their parents to help which was great. I couldn't stop there and talked with my teacher, Mrs. Castor, about earning a little money to donate to my mom's company. My teacher agreed to help.

During that week instead of spending time at recess, I did various chores around the classroom. I patted the chalk from the erasers, arranged school supplies, and swept the floor the best way I could. Anything the teacher wanted I made sure to do. Some of my classmates where so touched that they also joined in to do chores as well and told friends in other classes.

The teachers couldn't believe that a group of elementary school students all banded together so they could raise money and food for the homeless. To us it just made sense. People needed to eat and if we could help them, then so be it.

It was a few days before Thanksgiving and my teacher called me to the desk. I was cleaning out the Hamster cage at the back of the room and ran to her with a smile on my face. I thought she wanted me to do another chore.

"Myra, you have been such a hard worker this past week," Mrs. Castor said.

"Thanks Mrs. Castor," I responded. "Do you have anything else you want me to do?"

"No," she said and reached into an oak desk drawer. With a large toothy smile, she handed me an envelope and placed it in my small hands. "The other teachers and I are impressed with your classmates' hard work to help others."

I grabbed the envelope and looked at it curiously. I had received money before but it was always in a card or straight from the wallet. At the time, I didn't know what it was until she told me.

"Here is some money that we raised to reward you for your effort."

"Thanks," I said with joy.

"Thank you," Mrs. Castor said. I was confused and she could tell by my face that it showed. "For thinking of others."

"Sure," I responded. I took the money and placed it in my Trapper Keeper.

"Make sure to get this to your mother today. She's going to need the money so she can buy food in time for Thanksgiving."

"Will do Mrs. Castor."

My classmates came in after the bell but I didn't tell them about the money. I knew that would be stupid in case someone would try to take it from me. The day I received the money was great. I couldn't wait to get home. It was a beautiful and sunny day. The sky looked brighter because of my joy with having the money in my Trapper Keeper. Before going home, some of my friends told their parents. They where gathering stuff as well for the shelter.

Every day after work, mom would come home and greet my siblings and me. Then she would use the restroom and go to the kitchen for a glass of water. She pretty much did this every day and we would allow her to have a few minutes in the kitchen alone to relax with her cold five cubed ice glass of water. Sometimes I would get a glass for her and place it near the refrigerator. This time next to the glass was the envelope and I wrote on it 'five loaves and two fish'. After that, I went to my room and started on my homework.

Mom always came home before dad. He was a civil engineer and worked late due to a special project downtown. I heard her car and my heart leaped with joy. I wanted to be there when she saw the envelope but tried my best to hide the excitement.

"Hey mom," I said with a large smile on my face.

"Hello Myra," she said matching mine. Mom was tired and her eyes red. Probably stressed from work and trying to get more food. She told us the day before that she received some more funds so things will be tight but hopefully okay. After hugging me, mom talked to the other children, and then made her way to the bathroom and kitchen. I lagged behind a bit but couldn't wait to see her face.

"Oh my," mom exclaimed. She didn't even pour herself any water but counted the money in the envelope. "Where did this come from," she asked. I ran into the kitchen with my siblings.

"From school," I told her.

Mom was confused so I told her what happened. How I spent time to do odd chores in the classroom to raise money. My friends put all the money in one envelope. I didn't count the cash and just gave her all I had in my hands.

Mom hugged me with a tight squeeze. My siblings came over as well and we all embraced. She was so happy and that made me feel great. She told me that the money would be plenty for both the shelter and food pantry. Mrs. Castor was right about getting the money early. Mom said by having it early we could buy food that night and start preparing it in time for Thanksgiving. She was so excited about the gift that she brought us along to help with picking the food. When I was eight, I usually hated going grocery shopping. However, for that Thanksgiving I felt great because it was for someone else. I knew I wanted to help pass out food and this made that opportunity even better. It was one thing to serve, but it felt even better to help provide.

When dad got home, mom informed him of what happened and he was just as proud as she was. He was in such a good mood that he took us out to eat. The food was great but spending time with family at a restaurant was even better.

I was able to get out of school on the day before Thanksgiving. Mom rewarded me for my good behavior and said I could come with her to the office if I wanted. She didn't think it was a problem because we where going to get out of school early for the holiday.

When we arrived at the shelter, the employees and several other people greeted mom. I made sure to get out of mom's way so she could work. She gave me books and toys to entertain myself. Once the chance came to help, by filing papers or stacking forms, I was ready to work. Early in the day mom heard a few of the employees get excited because of something happening on the parking lot. She wasn't sure what it was and made her way outside. I stay by her side to see several delivery trucks pull up.

Many of these trucks where from various restaurants, grocery stores, and food warehouse places. Some even came from clothing stores and office supplies companies. The driver of the first truck in the parking lot asked for the owner of the shelter.

"Yes I'm her," Mom responded to the man.

"I have a delivery here for you."

"I didn't order anything," Mom said.

"It's on the house," the man replied.

Mom looked at me and I smiled back at her. "They came through," I whispered.

"Who?"

"My friends at school. They said they would ask their parents to help." I learned later that many of my friends had parents who owned various restaurants, grocery stores, bakeries, office supply stores, and clothing stores. They asked their parents to help and gave the shelter enough food to last through Christmas. The clothes were able to help those in the shelter and the office supplies helped save mom money so she wouldn't have to buy any for a year.

"You did all this," Mom said.

"Yeah, told you I can help."

******

"You see Penny; thanksgiving is more then just eating. But being thankful for family and helping others."

"That was cool grandma," Marsha says. Penny jumps at Marsha's voice. She was so engrossed in the story that she didn't notice her sister walk into the room.

"Thanks Marsha," I respond.

"I want to do that," Penny says.

"Do what," I ask.

"I want to help hungry people like you did." I smile and that brought a tear to my eye.

"Same here," Marsha says.

"Okay," I start, "after we finish the decorations and the meal, then I'll contact a local shelter or food pantry and see what we can do."

"Think they'll like cookies," Marsha asks.

"I'm positive."

If you do your part, God will complete the rest.

LUCKY?

Acts 20:6-12

The monotone professor talks endlessly about the importance of Tchaikovsky's influence on modern ballet. Being a physics student, Tchaikovsky is not an interesting subject. Sometimes it's cool looking at the leap of dancers and calculating their rate of ascent and speed. Outside of that, it's mostly a sleep-fest. For me, theory on Modern Ballet is the means to fulfill a general education course. Sheridan State University, forces everyone to take at least four of these general education classes. They use the reason so we can have a well-rounded education. I think it's to justify each department getting money from the University.

I should be use to it living in Sheridan Falls all my life. I could've went anywhere in the country but wanted to stay home. Not literally. I'm in a dorm with Earl who's from the Great Plains region of the country. Living in a coastal town you take some things for granted. Amenities like moderate weather, ocean views, lush plants, and even our own falls.

The town's name comes from the person who discovered the city and the huge 77-foot tall falls near the north side of town. Many visitors come for the beaches in the summer and travel north to see the falls. There are actually three of them but one is a main visitor site. The other two are a littler further to the north and not as big.

The ballet class is boring but I'm not alone. Earl is next to me sound asleep and snoring. I nudge him and he shakes himself awake. He kind of looks at me with a confused look and realizes that he's in class. We're in the back so it doesn't matter but I stop him before he gets to loud.

"Thanks Felix," Earl whispers. He straightens himself up and yawns.

"No problem," I respond. Earl is a mathematics student so his interest in the class is very low.

I wouldn't say that all non-science subjects are boring. Last quarter I took mythology, which was simply amazing. Earl said he enjoys French history and took the foreign language to match. I went with Spanish and took Latin American studies.

"Did I miss anything," Earl asks.

"Something about this guy wrote a ballet where this duck is both black and white and its importance on modern society."

"Shh," someone behind me says. I think her name is Julie. Not sure, don't really care. I thought she was pretty on the first day but she's very much into this class. Her name only comes up because she mentions it every time she answers a question. I assumed she was a dance major. She's not. I think its women studies but she takes every class serious as though it will save her life one day. Ridiculous.

"Sorry," I respond. A brief smile then my head turns to the front of the class. Earl nudges me and I look in his direction.

"Didn't that girl from Star Wars do a movie about that?"

"About what?"

"The duck or swan."

"She did a movie about a swan," I ask.

"Yeah. I heard she was good in that. Black something," Earl responds.

"Are you two going to talk the entire time," Julie whispers. Saying she whisper is a little incorrect. It was more like a quiet yell to get our attention.

The class is in a large 300-seat auditorium. We're not in too much danger of disturbing the professor. Besides, we're actually talking about the ballet. Sort of.

"We're in the back," Earl starts. "I thought this section was for the non-dancery students."

"Dancery," I laugh.

Julie rolls her eyes and looks at the images of ballerinas in various dance poses. Earl sighs but does his best to stay awake. Every now and then, he giggles over his dancery comment. The Professor mentions a midterm next week that causes Earl and me to look at each other in disgust. This class is not in either of our majors. That's fine because we decided to help one another in hopes of getting a passing grade.

Science and math comes easy for us but uninteresting classes, like dance, is tough. We leave the auditorium and the dance major behind us rushes by. Earl laughs and we keep heading out.

"They should show that film we where talking about, bet I don't fall asleep."

"It's rated R, doubt they'll play that," I respond.

"R?"

"Yeap."

"It's about ballerinas, how is it R?"

I shrug my shoulders. "Don't know, but it must have something in it."

We leave the building and take in the warm sun. It's spring so the air feels great against our face and arms. Earl is wearing shorts but I have the standard jeans on. Various people have the sea green and navy shirts. Our mascot, Shawn the Sea Eagle, is plastered on various shirts and hanging on banners. Its baseball season and many students are excited. I'm more into basketball but people just want to celebrate anything. So far, our baseball team is doing great this season and the campus newspaper keeps us on top of the news.

"What'chu doing after this," I ask.

"Hanging out with Suzie," Earl responds. Suzie is his girlfriend since halfway through autumn semester. It's his longest relationship in the three years I've roomed with him. Most of Earl's relationships barely last longer then the days between midterms. "You?"

"I have a Latin American History class, then some studying to do. Dynamics of Particles and Waves. It's pretty rough."

"I can imagine. Have fun. See you tonight."

We shake and he heads in the direction of Suzie's dorm. She lives on the other side of campus, which Earl hates. He doesn't feel like walking all the time but know it's worth it. Suzie is great and a positive influence on him. He studies more now that he's with her.

I have to unwind after the dance theory and Latin History class. Video games are the best way to chill so I play a fantasy RPG. I'm still surprise at the easy game play and graphics. I set my phone alarm so I don't go past a certain time. It's easy to do, especially when I get into a great part of the game and don't want to leave. However, I wasn't joking with Earl. I have a midterm next week in Dynamics and it's not that easy.

I can't say it's tough but certainly a class I need to study to maintain an A average.

After the alarm goes off, I look at the cell phone and roll my eyes. Can't believe it's time already. I kill one more troll and go to a place in the game to save my spot. I don't want to, but it's necessary. These books won't study themselves.

Three hours later of continuous problem solving, I take a nap and rub my stomach realizing its dinnertime. There wasn't anything in the fridge and living in a dorm I could've went to the cafeteria to get something to eat. That sounded okay but I want something different. Pizza and soda.

After placing an order with the pizza place, I make my way to the convenient store to get some soda and plan on picking up the pizza from next door. I threw on a light jacket because the temperature is cooler. Spring is one of those seasons where the day is hot and the nights cool. It's certainly my favorite of the four seasons. The pizza place and store isn't that far from the dorm hall so I decide to walk. I figure Earl will be gone for a while so I can eat this and make my way to the movie theater. Studying for three hours deserve a good reward.

On the way, I see a poster for a lecture from one of the professors about her life in the Amazon and meeting a missionary. The program sounds interesting. It would also fulfill a requirement in my Latin American Studies course. After thinking about it, I type the information in my phone.

While in the store, I have trouble. It's as if my mind cannot figure out which citrus flavored drink it wants. Orange or Lemon flavor. They're not the same but I stare at both intently. The store clerk is nervous. I keep pointing at both trying to make a decision. I'm glad various people walk in and out of the place while I'm deciding. Since I can't figure out which one, I flip a coin and orange soda wins. With that, I go to the clerk and bump past a sour smelling man looking at an aisle of chips.

"Sorry about that," I say. He doesn't respond and stares at the chips. Two people are ahead of me and I wait until both pay their money. Finally, it's my turn. The clerk rings me up and looks over my shoulder. I turn and glance to see what he's looking at.

The man who I bumped has a gun and is no longer looking at the chips. He's staring at us and glancing towards the entrance. The gun is wavering so he's either nervous or on drugs. Now wasn't a time for me to ask.

"Money," the man says, "all of it."

"Be cool," the clerk assures. He moves slowly to the cash register. I don't move. Not even breathe. "Be cool," he says again.

"Money," the man yells. "Move faster." He realizes that anyone could walk in and that could be trouble. I try to remember if there's a camera and how stupid he is for robbing the place with no mask. I'm sure the man doesn't care and really needs the cash.

Time crawls. Each moment feels like the tension filled seconds of a psychological thriller. The store feels quiet. The flickering halogen lights above are buzzing. Rare when you can hear that. The man's eyes are trailing to the side, which means the worker was getting the money out the register. I wonder if he wants mine as well.

"You want..." I begin and reach inside my jacket for the wallet. The guy gets nervous and scans his eyes back at me. He fires the gun five times.

Each sound of the bullet echoes through the convenient store with the intensity of a jet engine. The air shook and my ears trembles. The hairs on my arms stood at the possibility of pain and death coming my way. It doesn't take a Physics major to know that a piece of lead moving that fast at point blank range is lethal.

Instinct took over and I shut my eyes. A quick yelp shot out of my mouth and I jump back. Silence. I felt my body and wait for pain. My eyes open. I look around. For a moment, the gunman and I were perfectly still.

No blood. No wounds. No pain. I wasn't hit. I look at the gunman to see him looking at the ground. Five bullets lay perfectly still in a row. Each one next to the other in a straight line.

"Thank you Jesus," I whisper. The gunman is nervous and forgets the cash. He wants to shoot again but is confused like myself. He runs out the store and into a police officer walking with his partner. The man startles the officer who is not ready to breakup a robbery. They're probably coming in for snacks.

"Whoa," the officer says. He almost walks past the man until he sees the gun in his hand.

"Put the gun down now," the officer's partner orders. The man is nervous and surprised at the speed of Sheridan Falls' fineness. The initial officer grabs the man who drops the gun. He allows the officer to take him to the ground and get handcuff.

"Is everything okay," the second officer asks.

"He tried to rob me," the clerk yells. I nod. Both officers look at the bullets on the ground and then at us.

"Aren't you two lucky," the officer handling the gunman says.

"No, just blessed," I respond.

There are times that God steps in before you have time to pray.

TATIANA'S SACRIFICE

Judges 11

May 27, Sunday

Dear Diary,

Graduation is only a week away but I can't stop talking about it. To graduate from high school means more then just a new chapter in my life. It also means the ability to go to college and provide a better life for my family. We aren't in dire straights but with mom's death only two months ago, life has been tough.

Dad is a shell of himself. He was sick while she was alive, constantly suffering from chronic pneumonia. Mom was a great caretaker but her death really brought him down. I think the only reason why he keeps pushing is to see me graduate.

College and cheerleading are important so he thought to give me a diary so I can document my time in school. I'm happy and sad. Happy to move on to the next phase of my life and sad about no longer being the head cheerleader. To bad I didn't win Homecoming Court unlike the Queen at Brent. Out of all the years, Wedgewood would choose two nerds. Strange, but I was still Class Queen at the Senior Prom so that was great.

Speaking of Brent, I'm still upset over the school board changing the times for our girls championship basketball game. Granted I didn't play but it would have been nice to have a State championship while I'm at school, in any sport. I hope Carlton can deliver a championship while I'm gone and maybe he can talk his little brother into playing a sport. After what he did, there's gotta be some athletic skill in him.

I've seen movies and films on college life and hope to be a part of it all. Well, not everything. I can't get like some people and do radical dangerous stuff. But it doesn't mean I can't have fun and be a part of school activities. What am I saying, I mean college activities.

Mom was so helpful when I was picking a college. She made sure to ask the important questions to the admissions office. Plus, she talked with the various majors I want to study. She knew that my social life was just as important. I convinced her that through my social life I can build important contacts for the future. Especially with social media. The invention of Facebook, Twitter, Myspace, and various other sites has now allowed me to keep up with all my friends. I'm sure it's going to be even better in college and I can't wait for that time. It's going to be awesome.

Mark is a friend of mine since elementary school. He said social media would be great for us because we can keep up while we're at different schools. Whatever. Henry, the stud on the football team, is the one who sparks my interest. Too bad his girl, Rachel, is in the way. I shouldn't hate too much, Rachel and I are "friends" on the cheer squad. I can't remember which school Henry is going to. I know he got a scholarship for being a great player.

I really can't wait for the next phase. Not sure about dad. I'm a little concerned for him because the college I'm going to isn't in town. He told me that he will be fine and that I should go. If only Tim would help. In case you don't know, Tim is my brother. He's several years older then me and has no desire to go to college. He always says "Tatiana, you should stay here and help dad." I'm like why don't you help. Tim thinks his life is more important. Shame.

To Tim the only thing important is hustling to make a buck. He needs to be careful. A friend of his got caught trying to rob a convenient store with a gun. Some little store next to a pizza place. Shockingly he fired his gun and nothing happened. Strange. Tim told me the bullets laid on the ground. He must have been high, drunk, or completely stupid.

Tim sometimes does things, which can't be legal. I can't stand that because he has a few kids to feed. Technically, I shouldn't be hard on him. We where raised under the same roof and parents. I believe it's important to go to school and church, whereas he thinks that neither is good for him. Oh well, all I know is that I can't wait to walk across that stage and get my diploma. I've worked too hard for that.

May 28, Monday

It's Memorial Day, which is awesome. Some of my friends came over. That was fun. Dad seemed happy. Even Tim came over with my nephew and niece. Adam is three and Abby two. They're cute and it's great that Tim brought them over. For a brief moment, it felt like a family again. He wasn't over long but that's okay.

Dad was trying to grill but I told him not too. Mark came over and did that. He's like a culinary expert. Actually, I think he's going to culinary school. The food he grilled was fantastic. It felt great not thinking about anything but life, food, family, and enjoying myself.

May 29, Tuesday

Dad had a set back. The last time there was a holiday, mom passed away. I don't tend to look at Easter as a holiday like Memorial and Christmas. Probably because people don't take time off like the other days. It was tough for Dad during Easter and now Memorial Day.

The car accident Mom was in, only the day before Easter, was tough. We barely had enough time to say our goodbyes. Then on Easter, that was it. She was at rest.

Today Dad complained of breathing hard so I took him to the hospital. It's tough diary. Really hard to have to take care of him. He coughs so much. I see him struggling with the loss. It's hard on us all. But for dad, mom was everything. She's what he lived for. Mom, Tim, and I. Sometimes he complains of headaches and over all body pains. The one thing that keeps him going is my graduation. Can't wait for that. If only it would come sooner.

May 30, Thursday

Sorry I missed a day. Didn't plan on writing every day but dad is out the hospital. That's great. He's feeling much better. Sunday I graduate. Thrilled about that. I'm still concerned about his health when I leave. He assures me that he will be fine by the time I leave in August.

I think Mark, the guy who came over here and cooked the food, likes me. Oops. Didn't see that coming. Oh well, I was still glad he came over. He wrote me a note saying that he'll miss talking to me in study hall and wished he had taken me to prom. Weird. That was out of nowhere. I've known him since elementary. He's like a brother. Yuck. Glad I didn't tell him that. It would have crushed him. He's cute, but not my type. Athletes, that's what I'm looking for. LOL. Then again, what is my type? I'm eighteen. Not like, I'm ready for marriage. The only thing on my mind is summer break and college. And cheerleading. And fun.

Plus dad. And mom, I miss her so much.

June 3, Sunday

Graduation day. It was super awesome. All the girls where in purple and the guys in grey. I went to my friend's graduation yesterday and the girls were in white where the guys wore bright yellow. I forgot that it was tradition for girls to wear the lighter of the school colors and the guys to wear the other. I have to admit, I like our purple and grey better. It has a "je ne sais quoi" quality to it.

Dad was wonderful. He felt and looked like himself. He smiled more and laughed at the jokes from the speaker. I made sure to keep an eye on him from the stage. Tim was there, I think that made dad happy, plus Adam and Abby. They had no idea what was going on but cheered when everyone else did.

The graduation party was great. Dad called some people and apparently talked to Mark. They helped plan some things and Mark cooked some food. I'm shocked because his family had a party for him as well. Very thoughtful. He's going to a college near mine. I think it's like 30 miles away. Strange. I made sure to find out if he chose that because of me. He said he didn't. I believe him because of his scholarship. Full ride. Very nice.

There was an issue between Tim and me. We got into a slight argument when the company left. He wanted me to stay at home and help dad. That's what he thinks is best. I told Tim, that he lives in Sheridan and that he should help. You know he was difficult and made up some lame excuse that he has to take care of his kids. Which he does, kind of.

You see diary, they can't stay with their mom, because she's in prison for drug possession or something. That's messed up for their mom to be like that. If Tim was always with the children because of that, then fine. But Tim sometimes pass his kids to various girlfriends or random other people he knows. They stayed here a few times when mom was alive. That was cool but Tim really doesn't have much to do with Adam and Abby.

I only like him because he's family. I told him that. "You're lucky you're family, that's the only reason why I can stand you." That's exactly what I said.

Probably shouldn't have said that. I'll apologize in the morning. Sometimes I can be such an idiot.

June 4, Monday
   Dear Diary,
   It's me. I'm at the hospital. My dad and brother are both here. One because of the other.

   Tim went with some of his friends to do a drug run of some sort. I'm not sure if he went to buy drugs or transport them, but it was illegal. While he was out something went wrong. They got into an accident and two of them died instantly. Tim is in the hospital but they don't think he'll make it. I'm praying he does. Lord please don't let him die.

   Of course, dad heard about Tim's accident and that flared his pneumonia and heart condition. Now he's in one room and Tim in a different one. I can't lose both. I just can't. The last thing I told him, while he was conscious was that he was lucky for me to like him. Now look. I'm praying constantly in hopes that Tim and dad will live. I feel like I'm responsible for dad going through this. Even though it's not my fault.

   Adam and Abby was staying at one of their friend's place. It took awhile for me to find them. I had to go through Tim's phone and called the last few people he contacted. I couldn't tell the kids that their dad was in an accident, but told the people to bring them to the hospital.

   They're on the way. I don't know. I simply don't know how I'm going to tell them. When mom died, it tore me up and I'm eighteen. I can't imagine being three and two. What am I'm going to do?

   Funny, yesterday all I could think about was college, cheerleading, having fun, and social life. Now I'm hoping my family don't parish before this year is up.

June 5, Tuesday

Tim died. I can't stop crying. We weren't as close as we could've been, but I didn't want him to go.

Dad cried.

Now what?

Help me Lord.

June 10, Sunday

Last Sunday was awesome. I graduated and college was on the mind. Today, I buried my brother. Dad just got out of the hospital. He is weak. But alive. The kids are with us.

June18, Monday

Feels like forever since I wrote. Mourning is tough. In two months, I buried two of my immediate family members. Life is strange. All I could think about was college. Cheerleading. School. Getting an education. Now it's what will happen with Adam and Abby.

June 20, Wednesday

Hey Diary,

Mark is great. He took me to see a movie. I wasn't in the mood but he insisted. He rubbed my shoulder and told me that I'll be okay. He didn't try anything. That makes me feel good. Comforted. I need help. It's tough and I don't know what to do with my life.

June 22, Friday

There's a possibility that Adam and Abby will be split up. I can't have that. Dad is getting better but he's still mourning Mom and Tim. I talked to him. I hope he gets better. I can't have them split up the kids.

Dad keeps saying it's important for me to go to college. Feels like it's important. I agree, but family is everything. I can get educated anywhere. Adam and Abby might not stay as a family.

June 26, Tuesday

Mark went with me to the courts. He is such a great guy. Much more then a study partner. He came over Sunday and talked with dad while the kids where playing in their new room. Mark convinced dad that I couldn't do this alone. The courts will take those kids away. They're not going to trust their 18-year-old aunt, but with dad and me, then they will have a chance.

Dad kept talking about me going away to college. I understand that it's important, but I realized something. Family is even more so. There are still online schools or even some place here. Sheridan State is only down the street. Literally. But those kids cannot be separated. I can't allow that.

July 2, Tuesday

Last week the kids could have been separated. Now they will be in my care. I should say our care. Dad is much better. He even seemed more like himself. Staring at Abby, he sees Mom. At least that's what he told me. I can see the resemblance. Sort of. His coughs aren't as bad so he's not nearly as sick as earlier. I could still go away to college, but I'm not.

My entire senior year has been about going away. Having fun. Social life. Cheerleading. Partying and getting an education. Now I'm willing to sacrifice all that I thought was important, so Adam and Abby can have a family. Plus dad can live and live well.

Diary, Mark thought about staying to help, but I quickly convinced him that was crazy.

Did I tell you we're dating now? He's so awesome. Just think, Dad gave you to me so I can write about my life in college. Now it's different, but I'm glad I have this. Looking back has been interesting. I've learned. Grown. Definitely grown. That's awesome and I can't wait to see what's next.

A joyous life grows in love, relationships, and sacrifice for others.

JASON TEMPLETON

Genesis 39, 41

My name is Jason Templeton. Sometimes when you look back over your life you try to think of areas where you could change. Moments in time, that is altered by making a different decision. Correct a mistake that should not have happened.

One little decision and you feel like your entire life is ruined. Sometimes we believe and hope for the best. We cling to those moments hoping we continue to make choices that will be fruitful and positive. However, I began stating that there was a mistake, so my decision didn't have the positive results I was looking for.

For me the mistake, I would change, happened a few weeks before prom. Prom is a special time. It's a moment in a person's life that they never forget. You always remember that last dance or party as a senior in high school. The problem is that no one gives you guidance in the person you should choose. I should say your best friend or someone you genuinely like doesn't help you choose. Parents of course chime in. My suggestion for everyone is to pick your best friend. Do not go for the most attractive person you know, unless they are one in the same.

Marcy Sheridan is the person I should've chosen. Not because her name is the same as the town I live in, Sheridan Falls. It's because every since middle school we where always friends. Sure, the both of us are a little nerdy by our classmates' standards but that never bothered us. She has a little more Goth and I prep, but we got along. We always hung out, played video games, joined the chess team, and were each other's first kiss.

Being on the senior council didn't even change our friendship. I learned from Takashi to remain true to myself and if he, being class president, could take Claudeen from the special education class to a homecoming dance, then certainly I should have taken Marcy to the prom.

In spite of that, during the last quarter of school, I helped one of the cheerleaders, Cindy, in math. She was struggling and had to pass math or else she wouldn't graduate. I couldn't let that happen, so I agreed to help. Cindy was beautiful and way out of my league. She only asked because of my intelligence and growing notoriety at being the class vice president.

I didn't start the school year being the class V.P. It came due to an unreal event during our homecoming. Many of our senior class cabinet were removed from office for attempting some gross stuff to Claudeen. The rest of us on the cabinet took higher positions. The school administrators wanted to set a standard that being an elected official was a privilege. Not a right.

A month before prom, I decided to ask Marcy to go to prom. It only made sense and we had talked about it before. The day that I was going to ask her, I was tutoring Cindy. It came up between us that she didn't have a date for Prom. I was surprised. She was a popular student and well known cheerleader. Cindy was athletic and got a scholarship to a major school for gymnastics.

While we talked about prom, I was curious as to why she did not have a date. I assumed her boyfriend had just broken up with her, even though I didn't remember seeing her with one. Some people thought that she had other plans or was going to Wedgewood's prom. None of that was true.

Cindy informed me that she was waiting on me. That was weird and strange. There was no way a gymnast and cheerleader was waiting on a simple chess nerd. We talked for a bit more and my emotions got the better of me. I wasn't thinking about how I made a promise to myself that I would take Marcy. Instead, I asked Cindy and she accepted.

Fear and doubt replaced joy once Cindy and I stopped the tutor session. I went to see Marcy and realized that Marcy knew there was something I had to discuss with her. She assumed it was about the prom and would have been right had it not been for Cindy.

My best friend and I talked. Marcy could tell that I was avoiding prom talk until it came out that I was going with Cindy to the big dance. She was disappointed but we were not a couple, just best friends. The sadness in her face overwhelmed me. I could literally feel my heart tug as we parted ways from Martin's Ice Cream Shoppe.

The prom took place at a party room near the beach. It was great, peaceful, and fun. Lots of fun. There was plenty of socializing, dancing, and going down memory lane. At least 85% of the seniors made it and many juniors came because of their senior dates. It was great seeing some of the past pictures of various events throughout our four years. We went through the usual prom king and queen, as well as various other parts.

Marcy found a date. She took someone from another city who I believed is through her church organization. He was cool but you could tell they where just friends. The amazing thing is that I probably would've gotten jealous had I thought she was really in to him. Cindy was cool, but I didn't want to date her. She was arm candy. Someone to have and impress in pictures but not a person I wanted to be in a long-term relationship. I had a great time at prom but there was an ill feeling that I would look back and forget why I had even taken Cindy.

A few days before the prom, Marcy and I patched things up. We even took a picture together at the dance and decided to buy them for the memories. The both of us made sure to take this when our dates wasn't around. I'm sure someone might have told Cindy, but no one who cared about her was in the room when it happened.

After the prom, a group of us went to a black-lighted bowling center, which was weird. We where all dressed in tuxedos and dresses trying our best to bowl. I'm sure to the regular patrons it was strange but we where having fun. Cindy knew of a party that was going on at a hotel and begged me to take her. I agreed and we went.

The party didn't have the usual group of people I spent time around. These where the athletes and popular kids, I was use to the chess team and role-playing games students. I was happy that Takashi was there. At least he was someone I talked too. I spent most of my time with Takashi, but made sure to allow him to spend time with his date. I didn't know the girl but she was amazing. Sort of like Cindy.

The all night party was over and Cindy was ready to go home. We had fun and I had a great time with her. I agreed to take her home and walked her to the door. It didn't dawn on me to give her a kiss, even though we where on a prom date. The entire time I still didn't believe she was interested and assumed she was being nice for helping her with math.

Cindy was seductive and flirtatious. She rubbed my tuxedo and licked her lips. I knew what she was saying with her actions but couldn't believe it when she asked me to come in. I assumed her parents where at home. Cindy told me that they where out of town so the place would be empty.

Even when I went inside my mind didn't believe that anything serious would happen. Cindy on the other hand had other things in mind. I waited in her living room while she informed me that she had to change into something more comfortable. Cindy made her way upstairs to her bedroom and I ignorantly didn't think anything of her actions. That changed once she arrived downstairs in some sort of negligee.

My mind was split. The natural instinct was to go with what she wanted to do, which was now obvious. The other side didn't want too for two reasons. First, I thought for sure I should wait until marriage and not sin against God. Not to say I was perfect, but I knew this was something special. My parents and church members talked about waiting and how important it was. Especially since Cindy was not someone I was that close to. Physically attracted to, yes, but mentally connected, no.

That brought me to my second reason for not wanting too lay down with Cindy. Marcy was on my mind. If I had to lose it early, then I would prefer her. I know that might be sentimental or romantic, but I was serious about that. Marcy was someone I could at least say was worth it. Cindy was just some beautiful stranger. My relationship with Christ was growing and guilt was already tugging at my heart.

Before Cindy could trap me, I immediately ran out the front door. I could hear her call for me but didn't care. My first thought was to get to the car and leave. I was in such a rush that I forgot my tuxedo coat. The rational side of my mind thought it was wise to go back. The realistic part of my conscious knew that was a mistake. Besides, I could get it later. Cindy might be a little hurt but what does she care. It would be nothing for her to get someone else.

At school on Monday, it started like all others. A group of seniors all excited about coming close to the end of the school year. People talked about their time at prom and school went on as normal. That was until two uniformed officers walked into my civics class and arrested me for sexual assault on Cindy.

I explained and protested that they had the wrong person. I assumed that Cindy was attacked after I left and they where picking up the wrong guy. As I was being lead down the hall, I saw Cindy crying in the arms of a teacher. She heard me call out to her to tell the police officers that they made a mistake. Cindy knew that I hadn't assaulted her. She didn't say anything. My prom date kept crying and looked as though she was ashamed. Cindy had a stare that was both full of truthful revenge and lying betrayal. She knows she came on to me and nothing happened. That was crazy.

I spent the rest of the day with the police officers, my parents, and even a lawyer. I only admitted to taking her to prom, bowling, a party, and then back at her home. As soon as she showed up in a revealing outfit, I ran. Literally. I felt guilty and had to leave. I accidentally left my tuxedo jacket and I wanted that back.

The police were skeptical. What I was telling them sounded crazy but assumed that it was too strange to be a lie. However, since I was accused, they had to take the matter seriously. This meant that until they solved the case, I could not go back to Brent High. At the time, I was labeled as a sexual predator. The school considered me an emotional and physical danger to Cindy.

They delivered my schoolwork to me from school. Since it was towards the end of the year, then it wasn't as much of a problem, but still that was a hard time in my life. When I got home, I talked with Marcy who believed my story. She even agreed to gather my homework assignments and bring them to me.

Marcy assumed that Cindy was up to something. She figured it was revenge but tried to devise a plan to trick Cindy in revealing the truth. Marcy was such a great friend. Had I spent time with her after prom then I wouldn't be blamed for a supposed fake rape of someone I tutored for math. There was rage boiling inside me because I knew this would not have happened had I choose differently.

I have to admit there was a moment when I was angry with God. Who wouldn't be? I did the right thing and was still banished from school for a crime I did not commit. It would've been one thing had I started at her behest but then didn't stop because of her complaints. Instead nothing got started. I ran. Like Joseph. I ran.

Marcy vowed to clear my name, which was nice of her. I went over in detail, which hurt my soul, what happened that night. She wasn't listening for some warp enjoyment but to figure out the best plan of action. To get away from the mess, I went to Sheridan State University to hear a lecture on a professor's life conversion process. It was interesting and I believed I helped Marcy's brother, Felix, get a date with the speaker.

As always with him, he hates bringing up his name and its attachment to the city. However, he thanked me later for helping him.

That felt good, as well as inviting Marcy to the movies. We saw some action flick because I had to see something explode to take my mind off the situation. It was great sitting there next to Marcy. It felt right. There was a sense of compassion and unity with her. We sat on the beach and talked. It was liberating. Very open. I told her about Cindy and how I honesty felt. There was nothing there and especially no rape. She was touched how I felt about her and that I didn't mind admitting it.

This time we shared a passionate kiss. It didn't progress to anything else but that moment was very emotional. It was full of love and much more intimate then the stuff Cindy had in mind. Neither of us wanted to rush anything. We decided to become boyfriend and girlfriend and have the rest of our lives to take our relationship further.

Marcy learned that the Police was finished with the tuxedo jacket. There was nothing on it that proved or disproved me assaulting Cindy. I retrieve my jacket from the police while Marcy went to Cindy's home.

Marcy came back and was detailed about Cindy's conversation. The supposed arm bruises completely healed which meant that Cindy hurt her self to a point but used makeup to continue the lie.

Marcy planned to get Cindy in trouble and set recording device in various places of her home. I couldn't believe how she was able to do that and never really told me that secret. Cindy's home was large so there where multiple ways to get upstairs from various places from the main level. She used the knowledge I told her about the house and planted things around. She even asked Cindy about that night just to see if she could catch her in a lie but didn't.

It took a few days but Cindy eventually opened to her friends. We could hear through the recording device that it was a ruse and she used the lie to get back at me for making her feel stupid. Cindy was angry. She knew that I had feelings for Marcy and was upset that I didn't go as far as she wanted me to.

I assumed that Cindy chose me to help tutor because of my mind. I learned later that she had a crush on me since sophomore year. She couldn't say anything about it because of her cheerleader status but eventually overcame that and used the tutoring as a means to get closer.

She wasn't even bad in math. Cindy used that subject as means to get closer.

Running out on Cindy broke her heart. She felt worthless and was furious. The ruse that she came up with was out of anger and spite. I betrayed Cindy in her mind and ripped her heart out emotionally. Cindy was going to get even.

Marcy could tell that I felt bad. It wasn't as if I wanted to date Cindy but no one should have their heart broken I knew what it was like to be rejected. It's never fun and here I did it to someone else. She only came on strong because she knew that I wasn't going to date her for the long run. Cindy hoped that through a physical interaction maybe I would change my mind.

I told Marcy that although I felt bad, I still want to have my name clear. There was no way I could confront Cindy. I would have been in jail if I came in close contact with her.

Marcy was thrilled to confront Cindy. She knew my problem was because of Cindy so she wanted to end the charade of lies. Marcy went to school on a mission. She didn't want to blast Cindy on the paper or spread her business to the city. Since she had genuine feelings, Marcy desired to show a little compassion.

At home, I was waiting to see what would happen. I got a call from Marcy and found out that Cindy was dropping the charges. Marcy played some of her recording to Cindy and a few of her friends. They knew what was going on, but Cindy couldn't have the truth get out there. It would be devastating that she would have lied and tried to ruin someone's life.

I returned to school after the charges against me were dropped. It was just in time so I could graduate with my classmates and have my name cleared. My first thought was to be mad at Cindy, but I wasn't. I pulled her to the side and apologized. She was sorry as well for her behavior and we became friends. That was all. Nothing more then that. My heart was still for Marcy and there was no way I was messing that up. That's why I married her. It was the best decision I made. That and an idea to unify America.

The best means of dealing with temptation is to flee.

MYSTIC RIVERS

2 Kings 5:1-14

The auditorium is full and that's unexpected. I figured maybe 20 people might show up to hear me talk about my conversion to Christianity. The conversion took a long period of time, but Dr. Thomas Spitz thought it would be great to learn when I met a missionary as a young girl. Sheridan State isn't an overly religious school but he assumed some people might be interested. It fulfills requirements for various students in Latin American studies, and various other majors. That's probably why so many people are here.

"Dr. Mogesha, you all set," Thomas asks.

I look at him curiously and say, "You don't have to be so formal. Teresa is fine." For some reason when people are around Tom is very professional and likes to go by doctor this and doctor that.

"You know how I am," he responds.

"True."

"You seem," he starts then pause, "nervous?"

"Yeap."

"Why? You teach in rooms this size all the time," Thomas says.

I peek through the door from the hallway to look into a crowded auditorium. Strange. Even in some of my largest classes it's not this full save for at the beginning and finals. "I know. But it's different. That's about history and community concepts. This lecture is about me."

"You'll do fine," Thomas says. He gives me a hug and a large smile. I sigh and walk into the room. There is chatter when I walk into the auditorium. That makes the situation a little worst but I calm down and stand near the podium. The students, professors, administrators, and other people begin to get quiet. I recognize a few people from the two classes I'm teaching this semester but most are strangers. Thomas stands at the podium and begins.

"Tonight is a special night for our, 'get to know the professor', series during this semester. We have learned the jazz band exploits from one of our chemistry professors Dr. Yuri Henderson. We even got to know that Dr. Rebecca Springs from psychology visits her hometown of Greensburg Kansas to continue the repairs from the F5 tornado that devastated it. This semester we have heard from professors in music, art history, athletics, and engineering. Today we hear from Dr. Teresa Mogesha of the history department. She's a dear friend of mine and has a powerful testimony on her introduction to Christianity in the South American jungles. Please give a warm welcome to Dr. Teresa Mogesha."

There are some cheers and plenty of clapping. I shake Thomas hand and walk to the podium. I nod, sigh, and look into the eyes of my audience.

"Good evening," I start. There are various greetings and chatter. I laugh because many of my students know I start every class with a good morning or good afternoon. It's just habit.

"Usually when I stand up here, I'm talking about history of the Mayan, Inca, Aztec, or various other cultures. Today, as Dr. Spitz mentioned, this lecture, or should I say, talk. Is on history, but not ancient or far in the past," I say and there are a few chuckles. At least they're responsive. That's good. Hope they enjoy.

****

Villagers in the forest or jungle called me Teresinha. It's from that where my current American name, Teresa derived from. No one in the village called me Teresinha. I was known as Ters.

We lived near the borders of Brazil and Peru. Most outsiders came to our village and assumed that we didn't know anything about the current times or society. Our village was not as naïve like many people assumed. We heard of some tribes and villages that had little contact with the outside world and had a completely different lifestyle that resembled the stereotypes shown on TV. We chose to have our society and culture become a blend of modern and past influences. We were simple people, built around agriculture. Our village traded with the closest cities and made sure to have enough for our own. It was through this trade that various religious groups heard about us and made it their mission to convert.

For the most part, they failed. Many groups came in with their own assumptions on who we where and our lifestyle. They assumed that we where godless, uneducated, and ignorant of modern society. Some even thought we where cannibals which was far from the truth. Although some of my cousins used this lie to get rid of missionaries that where annoying.

Through the years from multiple missionaries, dad hated what they stood for. He didn't trust them and assumed that it was part of a larger conspiracy. I was young at the time so I wasn't sure if that was true, but I learned to trust his judgment. He was the chief of our clan and the smartest person we knew. His sons, my older brothers, where all warriors and held various power positions in the group.

When I was twelve, a new missionary came to the area. He didn't want to be a problem so he built a home near our village but far enough away that he wasn't intruding. He made sure to introduce himself to my father out of respect. The missionary didn't know our language but was familiar with Portuguese. Due to our interaction with the Brazilians, we had a variety of people who knew that language. Including my dad. However, dad didn't want the new man to know his bilingual ability so he spoke through an interpreter.

"Greetings great chief," the missionary started. "I am humbly Doctor Charles Norton. My wife Edith and I request permission to set up a small place just on the outside of your town."

"If it's on the outside, why do you request permission," my father responded through the interpreter.

"I have no desire to intrude or be an annoyance to you and your people."

Dad looked him over and at my brothers. The eldest shrug. The doctor didn't look like a threat. "Skill," dad asked.

"Medicines, healing," Dr. Norton responded.

"You can stay." There was a slight grumble from the side. Tocho, the area witch doctor didn't like any missionary who practice the healing arts. He felt like it was competition. Tocho hated to compete with outsiders.

"Thank you sir."

After the greeting, Dr. Norton left. We didn't see him for weeks. He was too busy setting up his home with his wife. He was smart to build near the river that had an endless supply of fish and freshwater.

51

Unlike those in my community, I was curious about Dr. Norton. Most of the other missionaries made their way constantly into our village. We knew what they wanted and how pushy they could get. Most of the time we would lie like we where interested and then eventually make it clear that our group wanted them gone. Dr. Norton was different. He hadn't taken one opportunity to come into the village. I couldn't stand it any longer and made my way to where Dr. Norton lived. It didn't take long to reach him and I saw the healing professional fishing in the water. He used a net to snatch up some fish and put them in a bucket. I hid from sight and shocked to see him return the fish he didn't need. Most people take more then necessary but he only took what was needed for him and his wife. Afterwards I saw him clasp his hands, bow his head, and whisper.

"Excuse me," I yelled. I was hiding behind a bush and step from behind it.

He jumped a little and smiled. I startled him. "Hello," he said in his best Portuguese. I could tell it was not his natural language, but it wasn't mine either.

"What where you doing," I asked.

"Fishing," he responded.

"No, after that."

The doctor paused for a moment and I could tell his mind was thinking. This meant that his behavior of bowing his head and whispering was very common.

"Praying," Dr. Norton responded. "I thank God for allowing me to eat one more day and for allowing this fish to give up it's life so I might live."

"Praying?"

"Yeap, praying," he said. He got out of the river and joined me on land. "Did previous people pray?"

I paused for a moment. He knew about others coming before him or at least assumed. "Yeah, but it was to teach us to change our, heathen ways."

"Sorry to hear that, but that's not me."

"I see."

Dr. Norton nodded and walked towards his home. I thought he was going to use the moment to convince me of his God. Instead, he walked to his home and waved goodbye. I can't figure out why he's here. I had to admit, I was curious and desired to learn more.

Over the next few weeks, I would meet with Dr. Norton. He would teach or tell me different things about his life. He was always polite and told me what he believed when responding to my questions. There was no pressure and I learned a different side of missionaries. It was intriguing and I have to admit would tell dad about the doctor's lessons. Dad didn't want me to hang around the doctor. However, my brother implored the Chief to let me go because I could monitor the new neighbor.

While talking with the doctor I was skipping rocks by the banks of the river. Dr. Norton was fishing as usual and paid me little attention. Then I slipped on a rock and fell. Nothing was broken but I was bleeding badly from my left hand. Dr. Norton saw me fall and quickly got out the water.

"I can help," Dr. Norton called out.

"I'm okay," I responded.

"Its okay, I can help," Dr. Norton assured me. He looked at my hand and ushered me to his home. His wife was there gardening in the back.

"Edith," Dr. Norton called out. His wife looked up and at our direction. "Get the clean water. She cut herself." Edith nodded and went into the home.

It was small but nice. The home used the materials around the area and some from the nearby stores. Some things where items he brought with him, but for the most part the house matched our own. Dr. Norton cleaned the wound with some clean water. It stung but was okay. Then he pulled out a brown plastic container. I wasn't sure at the time what it said and until he told it to me, but 'Hydrogen Peroxide' was something completely unknown that even saying it in Portuguese didn't make sense.

"This is going to sting a little bit, but it will kill any germs around the cut."

I nodded and held my breath. The clear liquid did sting and my hand bubbled. I snatched my arm a way but he assured me that it was perfectly normal. For a brief moment, it looked like my hand was possessed and was spewing white foam.

"That's letting you know that the germs are being killed."

"Okay."

He poured the clear liquid a few more times and the white foaming action wasn't as strong. Dr. Norton then cleaned the hand with some clean water and applied a gel to the cut. He said a word that didn't translated well, but it was 'Neosporin'. He informed me that it would help heal quicker and put a bandage on the cut.

After he did his job, the Doctor closed his eyes and paused for a moment. Something about it was similar to his acts while fishing. I bet he was praying but didn't say anything.

When I returned home, my hand wasn't as sore and it felt good. I even forgot about the bandage until my dad saw the hand.

"What happened Ters," he asked.

I looked at my hand and then at him. "I fell and cut myself. But it's better now."

"Where did you get the bandage?"

"Dr. Norton."

"Did he hurt you," dad asked.

"No, he helped." Dad was not convinced. He looked at my brothers and I could tell that he did not believe me. "He cleaned my wound," I said.

"We'll see. I will wait before passing judgment. Three days. You are not allowed to go to him during this time. We will check your cut after and see if he has truly healed your hand."

I agreed but felt bad for Dr. Norton. I'm sure after the three days he was wondering what happen to me. I didn't want to cast any suspicion on him so I stayed away. After the two days dad took my bandage off. He wanted to make sure there wasn't any foul play or tricks with my hand. Even Tocho was nearby just in case his services were needed.

Three days later the group gasped once the bandage was removed. They couldn't believe how well my hand looked. There was a slight line where you could see the wound but nothing remained.

"What magic is this," Tocho exclaimed.

"No magic," I started, "he just has this mystic water in a brown container and a special gel."

"I don't trust it," Tocho whispered.

"It worked Tocho," my dad said. With that, Tocho left the area angry. "You may see this doctor, he has proven himself useful."

Later that day I showed Dr. Norton my hand. He was happy with the results and curious as to why I stayed away. I informed him that my dad wanted to see his worth. He really thought that the doctor had done something to me and probably would have killed him. Removal was an option but not when it comes to messing with his youngest. Dr. Norton seemed relieved that the treatment worked and that he was not killed.

For the next few days, I started asking more about his God and belief. I was a little curious before, but now after my hand I desired to know more. He talked some about the simple aspects about God and His interaction in nature. That was interesting because it was as if he was grouping all my multi-god belief into one super powerful one. That made things easier to remember and understand.

My father got sick about three weeks after my own healing. Tocho did what he could with his practice. He used various plants, enchantments, dances, and chants to heal him. Nothing worked. Dad kept getting worst and he complained of stomach pains and feeling nauseated.

"What about Dr. Norton," I suggested.

Dad looked at me with doubt, but was willing to try anything. "Go and get him. See if his skills can help."

I ran as quickly as possible to Dr. Norton's home. Edith was there and met me.

"Is everything okay," she asked with a pleasant and concerned tone.

"It's my dad. Where's Dr. Norton?"

"He's out collecting flower samples for medicines, what is wrong with the Chief?"

I was curious about the flower samples but didn't have time to go into that. "He's sick and Tocho can't do anything about it. Dad has requested him for help."

While speaking, Dr. Norton walked up to his home and saw me talking to his wife. He waved and put his samples down but hurried over when he saw the concern look on our faces.

"What's the matter," Dr. Norton asked.

"It's my dad, he needs you."

Dr. Norton asked me to describe his symptoms so he could get the proper medication. He gathered some things and then followed me home. Many people where chanting and praying to the local god for healing. Even though Tocho wasn't helpful, he stood to the side murmuring some prayers and chants to heal the Chief.

Tocho saw us come into the tent and was not pleased. He rushed to Dr. Norton, Edith, and me. "Ters, why did you bring them here?"

"Dad requested him Tocho, now move." Tocho didn't believe me. He huffed at my comment but moved anyhow. There where too many people around for him to openly argue with the chief's child.

We entered the home and dad was still sick lying in bed. Sweat covered his body and eyes were glassy. Dr. Norton immediately began checking him in various places. He was gathering data and figuring out what was wrong. His eyes lit up and smile came across his face. Dr. Norton believed it was severe constipation, which was causing various other issues.

"We're going to have to clean you out," Dr. Norton said.

"What," my dad responded. He forgot that he was suppose to speak through an interpreter and responded back to the missionary. This did not shock Dr. Norton at all so he must have assumed that the chief could understand him the entire time.

Dr. Norton had some mixture of things and informed my dad to drink it. He even prayed over the liquid and gave it to dad. According to his face, it wasn't pleasant but he forced it down.

"Now what," dad asked.

"Stay near the toilet. Within an hour, the stuff I gave you should loosen you up and remove what's causing your sickness. Then I can get you something to fight off the remaining problems.

Dad was suspicious about Dr. Norton's plan. Then about thirty minutes later, dad immediately went to the bathroom and couldn't believe how the mysterious medicine made him feel. Dr. Norton even warned him that there will be cramping and some pain but once it's complete, he should feel great.

The time passed and dad felt much better. He looked drained but knew he was healed of his infirmity. Dr. Norton told him to bathe in the waters near his home and that he has some other treatments. The doctor told him to drink lots of water to flush out the remaining germs. The meds he gave my dad would help him out if he were careful.

Within a week, my dad was feeling great and perfect. This caused many people within the village to go to Dr. Norton. He did what he could and checked every single person. Some villagers actually needed surgery or more extensive help and he made sure they saw the right people in a small town in Brazil.

During this time people was asking Dr. Norton about his belief and God. Dr. Norton spread the message about his God but never forced it on the villagers. He was honest and just shared. Tocho wasn't happy because his own business went down but this didn't stop a few from using the witch doctor.

One day dad came to Dr. Norton with a gift. Dad gave him a few items that was precious and thanked the missionary for saving his life. He saw Dr. Norton pause over the drink and was curious what he was doing when giving him the medicines.

"I was praying," Dr. Norton said. "To my God for help."

"But you created the liquid medicine mixture," dad said.

"True, but I can only rely so much in my hands. Even at my best, I still need God to help. Human work will only get you so far, but with Devine power, then you'll never fail if it's according to His will."

Dad was moved by Dr. Norton's words. He desired to learn more about Dr. Norton's God. Dad was so impressed with Dr. Norton's words that he was baptized in the stream near the village. His conversion lead too many others also believing and a change of culture at the village.

We renamed the river to Mystic River because of the power of baptism in our new God, Jesus Christ. Tocho never came around and eventually moved to another village. He was appalled at the change but couldn't do anything to influence the people's mindset.

****

I take a breath and smile. After that, I talk a little about how I came to America to study and my road to Sheridan State University. There where some questions afterwards and the lecture is over. I talk to a few people and one individual was desperately trying to talk with me.

"Hi my name is Felix and thank you for sharing."

"No problem Felix. Glad you enjoyed the lecture."

"It was great; it really showed me how I should approach people from various walks of life. Thank you," Felix says. I can tell he's a student here but in none of my classes. Because I look like I'm their age, some time students approach me to go on dates. In reality I'm not that old, but am older then most of them.

"Felix Sheridan," a younger voice says from the side. A young man walks up to the two of us with a sense of confidence for someone to be a high schooler amongst college students.

"Hey Jason," Felix responds. He looks his way and then back at me. Then it dawns on me. Felix's last name.

"Did he say, Sheridan? Like the town and university."

"Yeah," Felix responds. I can tell that he's not ostentatious about his name being similar to the town of Sheridan Falls. "I'm related to the city founder, Brent Sheridan. That was in the 1800's so I don't tell anyone because it doesn't make me who I am today."

"I want to say that I enjoy your talk," Jason says and reaches his hand out. I shake it and nod.

"Thanks. It was a pleasure sharing."

"See you later Felix."

"Okay Jason, and how is everything?"

"Getting better. Marcy has been great," Jason says.

"Good to know," Felix responds and returns his attention to me. Jason leaves us and I can see him wink at Felix in my peripheral. I guess he did the last name thing on purpose to help Felix. I can tell that Felix didn't pay him any attention and had not planned to tell me his last name.

"Marcy is my sister. Our families are close."

"That's good. I can tell you don't want to talk about your family, but I am a historian."

"You want to know more," Felix responds.

"Don't want to be a problem, so if not..."

"It's cool. How about over pizza? I can tell you what I know."

"Sounds great," I say.

"If you think my family history is interesting, you should hear what happened to me a few weeks ago at a convenient store."

Strangers sometimes see God through your character and choices.

POWER OF ONE

I Samuel 14:1-15

Uriah Jackson, reporter and writer for the Sheridan Herald has an opportunity to interview local basketball star Mona Wilkerson. Unlike times past, Uriah is not only reporting for his newspaper but the local news channel as well. They are doing a story on various figures around the city and picked Mona for her choices on and off the court.

Most of the time Uriah would only have to worry about having his recorder and that there are plenty of batteries. Sometimes he even interviewed his people with his laptop and a microphone. This time he was using the cameras supplied by the television station. Uriah was thrilled to have the opportunity. He wanted to get out of the newspaper business and eventually launch into either TV or radio. This one time chance is what he was waiting for. Uriah's life would change due to a single choice by Mona.

When Mona strolled into the interview room, she did not flinch by the three cameras or the lights and sound people. The makeup crew already prepared her and the wardrobe was pristine. Mona wasn't use to the attention but took everything in stride. She already made her decisions on which college she was going to, so most of that burden was gone. To Mona, her decision that Uriah was reporting, wasn't a big deal but a way of life.

Uriah knew Mona was tall, but she was taller then expected. He had gone to a few games being a graduate of her high school, but never had the chance to talk with her up close. Other reporters at the Herald had their chances to do the interview. Uriah was chosen because Mona felt comfortable with his writing.

After the two said their pleasantries, Uriah described to her what was going to happen. He made it clear not everything would be used on the show. She figured that and was okay with that condition. Uriah told Mona that he would use their conversation in an article. Uriah planned to write the article and it would include more details. Mona was okay with the arrangement.

The following is a transcript of their filmed conversation.

Uriah: I am here with Mona Wilkerson, star of the Brent High Unicorns girls basketball team.

Mona: Thank you; it's a pleasure being here sir.

Uriah: Sir? You don't have to be that formal.

Mona: Oh, okay Mr. Jackson.

Uriah: Uriah is fine.

(Laughter between the two)

Uriah: So, tell me a little about yourself.

Mona: I go to Brent High, starting shooting guard for the Unicorn basketball team, single...

Uriah: Single?

Mona: Yeah, dated more as a junior. This year I was so focus on college and winning a championship that, I didn't make time.

Uriah: I understand, and besides you have you entire life before you.

Mona: True. Didn't think about it like that.

Uriah: Have you always played basketball?

Mona: Amazingly, no. My first love was gymnastics. Then I got tall.

(Both people laugh)

Uriah: You don't say. Is that when you turned to basketball?

Mona: No sir. Tennis

Uriah: Explains your incredible stamina.

Mona: Yeah, most people don't realize that, and eye-hand coordination. Gymnastics allowed me to be flexible and build strength, while tennis helped with other things. Then I started liking basketball, but I've never given up on playing tennis.

Uriah: Wimbledon?

(Mona laughs)

Mona: No, not at all. Only for fun and exercise. I tell many of my teammates to pick up other sports. It makes you a better athlete.

Uriah: Any of them listen?

Mona: Yeah, especially this freshman. She's the sixth woman on the team. Ocean.

Uriah: Ocean?

Mona: Yeap, like the bodies of water. It's different I know, but she's a great person. She picked up tennis and martial arts. A young guy at Wedgewood is training various high school students from both schools.

Uriah: Speaking of Wedgewood, a special thing happened last week.

Mona: It was great. The game...

Uriah: Before we get on the game, let's back it up a week.

Mona: Okay.

Uriah: It's a week before the state finals. Something amazing happened. Two teams from the same city are in the state's final four.

Mona: It was pretty exciting. Especially since Wedgewood and us don't get along. In sports. Off the court, most of us aren't enemies.

Uriah: Why is that?

Mona: We all live in various areas of the city. My dad told me that Sheridan Falls city school district wanted to make sure there wouldn't be any problems. They knew if they draw a dividing line through the city, it would cause issues and fights. So, they cut the entire city in various parts that way both Brent and Wedgewood students are spread throughout the town.

Uriah: Sounds like a perfect plan.

Mona: It keeps the fights down. Don't get me wrong there's passion on the court when the whistle blows.

Uriah: Your passion leads you to a very important decision. What was it?

Mona: To be honest, I didn't realize that it was that important. Actually, it is something I've done all year long. During my freshmen year, I started worshipping on the Sabbath.

Uriah: Sabbath?

Mona: Yeah, we worship on Saturday and keep that day holy.

Uriah: Like Jews?

Mona: Something like that, but we're still Christians.

Uriah: Continue.

Mona: Because of that, I have chosen not to play basketball Friday evening until Saturday evening. Different people do various things, but that's what I choose to do for God.

Uriah: Nice.

Mona: Even some of my friends who go to church on Sunday have been keeping various periods of 24 hours in dedication to God.

Uriah: Interesting. I think BYU teams do that.

Mona: You're right they do. That's where I got the idea.

Uriah: Have you always gone to church on Saturday?

Mona: No, I've been doing this for a few years now. There have been games that fell during that time, so I wouldn't play. Coach knew about it, and my teammates. Some games were changed or move. I made a commitment to God, that no matter what, I would do this for Him.

Uriah: Including the state finals.

Mona: Including that. This is why I didn't think anything of the championship game being on Saturday. Of course, we had to win the semi-final before making it to the finals.

Uriah: During that week, everyone assumed you would win.

Mona: I didn't, but knew it could be an issue. My teammates knew that I wasn't going to play. I was cool with it and most of them where as well.

Uriah: Some wasn't.

Mona: I would imagine, but then again I'm guessing. I really don't know. No one said anything to me at the time or since.

Uriah: What was happening behind the scenes?

Mona: You mean my coach working on getting the time change? Yeah she was working hard. This was funny to the state board, because we hadn't even won yet. They really didn't want to commit to a time that was convenient for one player, just in case I couldn't make it.

Uriah: So your team was okay, what about others? Was everyone cool with the possibility of switching times?

Mona: I remember when the Herald interviewed me about playing in the state final four. I was excited and said we couldn't wait. I guess the reporter knew about my religious belief and asked. That's when it got out and hit Twitter and Facebook. Then everyone found out about my beliefs, which was cool, but the hate and love messages came.

Uriah: Hate and love?

Mona: Yeah. There where many people who supported me.

Uriah: Brent High fans.

Mona: Yeah, and some on the other side. Many people thought it was important to stand up for something. Often we don't take notice until there's a sacrifice involved.

Uriah: That's an interesting thought.

Mona: It's true. For example, some people donate hundreds, thousands, and millions of dollars to various charities. We think it's big, special, and important. But most of the time, they have so much money that it barely hurts their bank account. However, you get others who donate 50 bucks to their church for a special project, after they've already given their usual tithe and other things to the church on a limited budget. To them it's all about making a sacrifice. Showing God you're serious and not playing church or just being religious.

Uriah: That's serious.

Mona: I'm still young, have some growing to do. I choose because I felt like God was leading me there. So, even if I were by myself, I still would choose him.

Uriah: All that week, there was anticipation if you would play but first the other games were played on Thursday.

Mona: Correct.

Uriah: What happened?

Mona: We beat St. Katherine's and Wedgewood was victorious over Franklin High. That set up an unreal match up between two high schools from the same city.

Uriah: Now that it was real, how where you treated?

(Mona pauses)

Mona: It was tough. Because many people from Brent got on me because they didn't want to lose to the cross-town rival. Where as Wedgewood students where on social media stating that I should make God more important and not play.

Uriah: Of course.

Mona: Yeah, it was weird. Wedgewood did not want me out there because it would mean their first championship in any girl's sports. Their main player, Pam....something was thrilled with my decision.

Uriah: Pamela Silvers?

Mona: Yeah that's her. She wanted to play me, but really didn't.

Uriah: The star of Wedgewood.

Mona: True, this is why she did not want me there.

(Both people laugh)

Uriah: What changed?

Mona: Coach Clayton was working hard behind the scenes with our administrators to have the game pushed. Apparently, nothing was going on at the time, so there wasn't an issue. The board didn't know if they should make that change, but heard about how I have been the same the entire season. I was consistent and they admired someone standing up for something they believed strongly in. They thought it was nice for me to take on a rule or an organization because of personal conviction.

Uriah: And then it happened?

Mona: The school board came out and stated they would allow the game to start right at dusk on Saturday. I was very surprised. My mind was set on not playing. It wasn't even a question. I was going to face that temptation head on and win.

Uriah: The school board makes a change.

Mona: Yeah.

Uriah: Now you can play.

Mona: Yeah.

Uriah: Did the reaction change?

Mona: Definitely. Some of the same people who was chastising me and stating I should forget my convictions was now saying how proud I was for standing strong.

Uriah: Interesting.

Mona: That's people.

Uriah: What about the Wedgewood side?

Mona: Pam didn't hold back. She hated that one person could change the time of a game. It's not as if they changed the rules for me to play, or the dimensions of the court. The time of the game was arbitrary. I didn't see anything wrong with it.

Uriah: It's dusk on Saturday. How are you feeling?

Mona: Thrilled. I get to play. Especially since I didn't think, I would.

Uriah: Did you pray? Ask God to get them to change?

Mona: No.

Uriah: Why not?

Mona: I love Him. I love God. What I was doing was an act of me showing love for Him. I didn't want to change the parameters of the relationship that had been established. To me it was simple.

Uriah: For all those who may not have known, what happened next?

Mona: We won. It was close. But we won.

Uriah: Champions.

Mona: That's right. Champions.

Uriah: Can't take it away.

Mona: Not at all.

Uriah: How do you feel now?

Mona: Like it was all worth it. It's cool to show people what the power of one person can achieve.

With Christ, all battles are winnable; we just have to be willing to show up and believe.

AND THEN CAME A STRANGER

Luke 8:41-56

School is over and now it's time for summer and shopping. I'm here at the Valhalla Mall with my two best friends from middle school, Hillary and Ocean. We're excited at moving to the next stage of our lives. High school. We came to Valhalla to check out some of the latest styles for this upcoming school year.

Strange, Valhalla is the name of the mall, but the entire shopping district has Norse sounding names. There's a Loki street, Odin shopping district, and Feurir's entertainment area. There are others but I forget their names. Valhalla mall has a huge center foyer with three massive halls streaming from the middle. Each section has its own anchor store that covers both floors of the mall.

"Cecilia." I snap out of my daydream and look over at Ocean. "You were out of it," she says.

"Thinking about school," I respond.

"We just got out for the summer," Hillary says. Her face is covered in disgust.

"Not Hubert," I respond. Hubert is our former middle school. Home of the Tigers. Black and orange was everywhere. Even the hall next to the gymnasium has a large Tiger painted on the side. "I was thinking of Brent." That high school's nickname is Unicorns. Ocean and I are excited to go there together.

"I can't wait," Ocean responds. "Think I'll start?"

Ocean was the star basketball player on the Hubert girls team. Every since she could throw a ball in the hoop she wanted to play in college. She doesn't have any schools in mind but can't wait to play for Brent High.

"You'll be a freshman, who knows," I respond.

"True, plus they're pretty good," Ocean responds.

"Like really good," Hillary emphasizes. "Don't they have that star on the team?"

"Mona," Ocean starts, "Yeap. She's amazing. This year is her last and colleges from all over are trying to get her to commit."

"You're going there too," Hillary says and looks at me. I nod. Brent sounds fun and I'll go on their cheerleading squad. The middle school didn't really have cheerleading. Not for real. I played some ball, but that wasn't my thing. I really wanted to do other things, but it was a cool way to spend time with Ocean and Hillary.

"You're going to that academy," Ocean asks Hillary.

"Yeap."

"That's pretty far, isn't it," I ask.

"It is, but not that bad. It's not like I'll never see you again." We all laugh. "The choir is going to your church."

We finish eating and collect our trash. "My church? Choir?"

"Yeah, don't you go to Victory Praise Temple," Hillary asks.

"Yeap."

"The boarding school I'm going to have a traveling choir that goes to churches and places throughout the summer. It helps build attendance and notoriety for the school."

"That sounds cool," I respond.

"I know right, tell me how they sound," Hillary says.

We throw away our stuff and ignore a group of boys from the area middle school. They try to look tough and smooth. The tallest one tries to ignore us but I can tell by the quivering grin that he likes me. We laugh a little and keep walking towards the clothing store.

"They'll follow us, watch" I tell the two.

"You think Marsha is going to be okay," Ocean asks. She has a one-track mind sometimes. If it's basketball then it's hard for her to leave that conversation. If she's thinking about science then it's that. If it happens to stray to computers then that's all she talks about. Whatever is important at the time to Ocean that's where her mind stays.

"She'll be fine," Hillary responds. Marsha will be the new star on Hubert's girls basketball team. She loves playing ball and baking cookies. Kind of an interesting mix but she loves sports about as much as Ocean.

"Besides she spent as much time in the gym as you," I tell Ocean.

Hillary and mine name came from our parents liking the way it sounds. They looked it up and liked the meaning as well. Ocean is different. Her mom really likes the water. An Uncle of hers is an adventurer and another one was a Navy Admiral. Ocean's family goes on cruises at least once a year, and her parents go all the time without the kids to celebrate their anniversary. Their family loves the water. Except for Ocean.

Ocean is not a great swimmer. She's afraid of drowning and gets seasick every time her family goes on a cruise. She even has a weird phobia of large-scale aquariums. Never heard of anything like that before, but she's the complete opposite of her name. It wouldn't surprise me if she changes it. I doubt it. Once she is known in the college basketball world, you cannot change such a unique name.

"I think you're right about those boys," Hillary tells us. I look around and the guys are following behind from a distance. We giggle some and walk into the all girls store. If they follow us in here, then I know they're interested.

"Told ya," I respond.

At church, I wait patiently for the choir Hillary spoke about a few days ago. I see them listed in the bulletin and excited to hear them. Never saw myself as a great singer, but I dabble in the performing arts.

Even at Hubert, I was in a few plays, sang in the choir in seventh grade, and did a poetry reading for my class. It was weird. I get stage fright, but I do like having the immediate attention. It was easier then playing basketball. I couldn't believe how often the coach wanted me to go in sometimes. It's not as if I was great

Pastor Tyrone is cool. He's new at church but is really doing things for the young people. He has programs, group discussions, and various other events geared for us to enjoy ourselves at church. Just earlier they where talking about a summer camp. Not sure if I want to do that. It sounds okay, but I want to have a good summer preparing for the next stage of my life. Have to make sure that I wear the proper outfit and looking great for my first day at Brent.

To my far left is Sam. I've known him since going to Victory. I think he's in my school as well and hangs out with Marsha. He nods and gives me this weird smile. I quickly return the favor and look at my bulletin. He's different, shy, and quiet. Not qualities I like in a guy, but at least he's harmless. Besides, I think he's in 7th grade so he's only going to the eighth. I decided that I will only look at high school guys. Can't wait.

The choir from Hillary's future school stands and get settle in the choir pews. They sing a marvelous version of "Amazing Grace". They sing it in a unique style and completely memorable. They sung another song call "What If God" and then "Alpha and Omega." Even during the sermon, I keep thinking about the choir. They look like it was so much fun. After they sang, the director mentioned that they still have enrollment spots at the school whether you're a singer or not.

I never thought about going away to boarding school, but it sounds like fun. It's not nearly as big as Brent is, but the experience will be amazing. I think about the opportunity to sing in a traveling choir, if I can make it, will be delightful. I have to get over my stage fear that pops up. What to do?

After church service, I head to the boarding school's table. I tell my mom about my desire to go. She's surprised and supports my decision. Dad seems cool with it as well. I don't know how much it will cost but positive it's expensive. I have no desire for them to go broke for my high school tuition and later for college. That's insane when a perfectly free high school is in town.

At home, I talk with both parents and my desire to help with any tuition cost at the boarding school. They're surprise. I tell them I'm serious about going and am willing to pay for it.

"How about you sleep and pray about it," dad suggests.

I agree. Sometime we make rash decisions based off emotions. That's not a good idea with something as important as education. I agree with him and decide to pray. They both give me their blessing and will support any decision I make. I can tell by their tone that they assume I wouldn't go. I pray, sleep, wake up, and give my decision.

I'm going.

I send a text to Hillary and Ocean informing them about my decision. Both say the usual congratulations and it feels great. The plan is to get jobs and find means to pay for tuition. The only question is how.

Two weeks later, I meet up with Hillary and Ocean at Martin's Ice Cream Shoppe. During that time, I've done a lot of babysitting, gardening, babysitting, clean houses, and more babysitting. It was tough and I didn't get to see Hillary or Ocean that much but gathering the cash made it all worthwhile. I also haven't spent money but figure to splurge so I can see them. Splurging isn't really that much since I plan to get a single scoop sundae.

The two are already there and waiting to the side. Neither have ice cream, which is cool. I'm glad they waited. Surprised, but happy they waited. I smile, wave, and walk towards them.

"Hey."

"Hey stranger," Hillary says. I mock her and sit down. Ocean is quite. Her body language is rigid and almost like, there's a wall between us.

"What's the matter," I ask Ocean.

"Nothin'," Ocean responds. "Ready for ice cream?"

Before Hillary and I respond, Ocean gets up and heads to the counter. We both look at each other confused. "What's with her," I whisper. Hillary shrugs.

We order our ice cream and the conversation is stale. Hillary and I are cool but Ocean is quiet. Unusually quiet. At least if she talks about basketball, she's talking.

"Ocean, what's up," I ask. Ocean pauses while eating her sundae and then puts the scoop in her mouth. "You came here to look at Hillary and I talk," I continue.

"You and Hillary," Ocean mocks.

I look at Hillary and then back at Ocean. "What's with you?"

"We where suppose to go to the same high school. We all where," Ocean responds.

"So what's the problem," Hillary says. She's not as perceptive, but I see where Ocean is going with this.

"First you break up the group by going to that snooty school," Ocean says to Hilary. "Sorry we all can't be as rich as your family."

"That's a good school Ocean. I'm not going there because of money."

"Then you convince Cecilia to leave and join you."

"No she didn't," I respond.

"She went on and on about the choir and stuff coming to your church. I knew what she was doing," Ocean says as though Hillary wasn't there.

The argument continues like this between Ocean with Hillary and me. We are trying to convince her that this wasn't a conspiracy. We didn't think of this plan to make her mad by going to the same school.

Hillary was surprise that I wanted to go to the boarding school. She figures I would stay at Brent High because of the people I knew there. Going to Brent means that I would come in to the situation much better then the normal freshmen.

One of the clerks came over to our table and tells us to quiet down. I feel embarrass because some people are staring. We eat a little more but Ocean can't. She stares at her dessert and then looks our way.

"I thought we where a team," Ocean says and gets up from the table. Hillary and I are confused and watch her leave the Shoppe. While she was leaving, Marsha was entering and didn't get many words from her former teammate. Marsha is with her cousin and sister Penny as they walk into the place. She looks over and wave at us. We respond the same.

"I didn't realize she was so mad," Hillary says.

"You've been around her more then me these past two weeks. What happened?" Hillary shrugs. We eat a little more. "I need some better paying jobs."

"Its tough, we're coming out of middle school."

"I know. Too bad I can't use my skills in performing," I say.

"You have terrible stage fright," Hillary laughs.

"That's before I go on stage. Once the performance starts, then I'm fine."

"I don't want to interrupt," Marsha says. Her voice startles me. Marsha's cousin is paying for their desserts. Penny is licking her mint chocolate ice cream scoop with enthusiasm.

"Hey Marsha," I respond. "Its okay, how are you doing?"

"Great. Getting ready to go to the Rockies."

"You moving," Hillary asks.

"No," Marsha starts. "Just spending the summer there. Did I hear you say, that you wanted a chance to perform?"

The next day I arrive at an audition for a summer play. They need a variety of actors of various ages but most of us where young at the summer playwright program. That was cool because the plays would change every three weeks. I can't believe that Marsha knows about the audition and its location. I guess some friends of hers on Facebook talked about it and she had thought about going herself. She didn't want to perform and will be in the Rockies. Marsha did bring some cookies to the theater because she likes baking.

The pay wasn't fantastic but more then I was making doing the odd jobs. Not to say I wasn't still taking baby sitting jobs but it's different. I enjoy acting and tell some of my clients where I was performing. Many of them brought their friends, co-workers, and church friends to the plays. This brought in more money and made it fun.

The stage fright never went away. Always before a performance, I would feel like throwing up or passing out. After a few deep breaths, a swig of water, and shaking myself, I was good to go. Hillary came to one of the performances but Ocean never wanted to show up. For many weeks, the three of us never really talk that much. I should say that Ocean and I never talked that much. For some reason she was mad at me compare to Hillary.

Ocean understood why Hillary went to the boogie school as she calls it. Hillary's family had more money then the both of us. Ocean is disgusted with me because of how hard I'm trying to get in the boarding school. In reality, my family could make sacrifices and pay for it but I didn't want that. I had to come up with some of the money and learn some responsibility.

On one of the days I have a break I visit Hillary. We talk and get on some online chat rooms. Mom drops me off and I wave her good bye. Hillary answers the door and is not pleased.

"What's wrong," I ask her.

"Guess who's having a birthday party and we're not invited," she responds.

I pause for a moment as I lay my laptop down on the table. "Ocean? It's Ocean's birthday," I exclaim.

"And she's having a party."

"I didn't see anything about it, not even on Facebook or twitter."

"She went old school and invited people with cards and in person," Hillary responds. She's red in the face and frustrated. "We've been her friend for years. What's with her?"

"I can't believe she's this angry that we're going to the same school. Not like we're going to stop being friends."

"I know right."

I sit and sigh. Hillary's couch is extra plush, but today it feels normal. "We've been BFF's for years. I figure we'll always be like that."

"I know right," Hillary says again, this time with a slight break in her voice. She's starting to tear up and I can't have that. If she cries then I'm definitely crying.

"Where's the party?"

"Remember that place by Valhalla. That little party time place thing."

"Yeah," I say. Amazingly, I actually remember the place that Hillary is referring too. It's new, almost like a restaurant and video game entertainment center but different. It has a section for adults, plus a side for young adults and children. Instead of an extensive menu, it has pizza and wings. There are play-pins for younger kids, but various games and other entertainment fun for us young adults. "Wanna crash it," I ask. Hillary nods emphatically.

We take bikes up to the mall. Hillary doesn't live that far from it so it's convenient. I have to ride her brother's bike. I know him and he's nice to me. Besides, sometimes he stares. I know he's going to Brent and will be a junior there. But every now and then mumbles something about me going through the changes. It's weird because many guys do it.

Hillary and I arrive at the party. I get that same nausea feeling, dry tongue, and slight dizziness. Hillary watches me breathe slowly and then shake. "I'm ready."

"Okay," Hillary laughs. We chain our bikes to the rack and go inside.

There where several people we recognize walking about. At least twenty. Hillary has to be as disgusted as myself. Can't believe Ocean would do this. I should take her on a boat and leave her. No that's mean. I'm frustrated, not vindictive.

, "There she is," Hillary says. I could see the back of Ocean as she talks with some friends. They are all on the basketball team so I know them, but we are not close friends. Ocean is tall for her age and looks like she's growing taller. Both Hillary and I come around her chin, but that didn't scare us one bit.

I tap Ocean's shoulder and wait for the surprise. She looks around and gives me her large eyes, gaping mouth, and a long pause. I smile.

"Happy birthday," Hillary says in a very sarcastic tone. I didn't want trouble, but knew Hillary might accidentally start something. Even though I doubt Ocean would fight us.

"Hey," Ocean starts.

"Why didn't you invite us to your party," Hillary shouts.

The room for a moment went silent and then back to the usual noise. Most people knew we where friends so no one thought anything of us getting a little loud. Like regular friends, we argue and laugh.

"I'm sorry," Ocean says. Her shoulders slump and she looks around embarrassed. "I thought you wouldn't want to come."

"Are you crazy," Hillary says. Her voice isn't as loud as before. "We're BFF's. I look at you like my sister." Hillary's voice breaks up some. There she goes with the almost crying.

"Can we go some place away from traffic," I suggest. Shockingly, Ocean doesn't suggest that. They both nod and we go to a different area of the 'fun time' place. Hillary pulls herself together and takes a few deep breaths. Then she shakes herself and looks at me with a grin.

"Ocean, why are you acting like this," I ask. There's no reason to use her name. She can see me look at her but I want to drive the emphasis of how ridiculous her behavior has been.

"I thought you two where leaving me. Didn't want to be my friend anymore."

"Why," I ask.

"Because you're going to a different school than me."

"So we're going to a different school, that doesn't mean we will stop being friends. We have all the means in the world to keep up with each other," I say. "Plus you can keep us up to date on what's going on here."

"Besides," Hillary starts, "we're only going to be fifty miles away."

Ocean stares at the both of us. Then she glances at the floor. "I'm sorry."

"It's okay," I respond. "We all do weird things."

"And will continue too," Hillary says and laughs. We all give each other a hug and start to tear up some. It stops when some random guys our age make a joke about them liking us hug one another.

"Boys are so immature," Ocean states.

"Yeah, glad I'm a girl," I say.

The rest of the time was great. We all spent time with each other and the various people from school. All three of us attend separate churches so some of Ocean's religious friends are here. It was nice meeting other people and had a great time.

A week after Ocean's birthday party she comes to one of my performances. We where doing a performance on one of Shakespeare's play "The Merry Wives of Windsor" except in our version it's the "The Merry Teens of Sheridan". People seem to like the humor of the play, which is great. Ocean is surprise and thinks I did a great job.

It's getting close to when school will start. I have a huge chunk of money to go and my parents are thoroughly proud. They can't believe how hard I worked just to earn my way into the school. Later today, mom is going to call the school and put the money down for me to go.

I spend some time at the courts with Ocean so she can practice her jump shot. She's nervous about making the team but I assure her that she'll be fine. Can't promise she'll start but I know she will be on the team.

My brother Gene was on the far court playing with his friends from high school. It was cool of him to bring us along. I know he didn't want too, but it was still nice. One of his friends is cute and I believe he thinks I'm cute, but I know Gene is not having any of that. He does not want one of his friends dating his younger sister.

While shooting and talking with Ocean I hear a loud thud and scream. Neither of us pays attention figuring someone is either fake hustling or just got fouled. It's not until the guy I think is cute calls my name. I look over and my heart leaps at the sight.

Gene is on the ground and trying to stand with blood pouring from his mouth. I froze for a moment and then run to the court. Ocean is faster then me and beats me over to my older sibling.

"What happened," I yell.

"Gene ran, was going for a dunk, tripped, and fell into the pole," one of the guys says.

I see blood on the pole, my brother, and the ground. Little white things where on the ground around him. Teeth. They where pulling him up so he could stand but he seems dizzy so I motion for them to put him down again.

"Concussion," Ocean whispers.

"Yeah, I know," I whisper back.

One of the guys is on the phone. He calls 9-1-1 because it's automatic. Gene says he feels like his head is spinning so calling the emergency crew is the best thing to do. I call mom and tell her what happened. I talk to Gene and assure him everything will be better then okay. He nods and tries to stand but this time we all keep him on the ground.

Another ball player runs back from his car with a shirt. He motions for Gene to press it against his mouth to slow the bleeding. Mom is nervous but I assure her it's going to be okay when the sirens from the ambulance are heard in a distance.

The emergency crew takes Gene to the hospital while Ocean and I follow along with the cute guy in his car. Its small but he gets us to the hospital safely. He hangs around, that's nice, and mom meets us there as well. It doesn't take long and they check Genes for any bone fracture as well as concussion. Through the panic, one of the guys and Ocean picks up Gene's teeth. Because of that, they might be able to implant them back into his head or he'll have to get new ones.

Mom and dad are worry about their son as well as I. Can't believe that Ocean hangs around but she does. She even tells Hillary who was with her family at an amusement park. We could have gone but it was a family reunion and neither Ocean nor I wanted to go.

"Don't worry about money," I tell my parents.

"What," dad asks.

"I know we have insurance, but you'll still have to pay some of the cost." Both of them nod their heads. They're a little confused. Understandable. "So don't worry about it, I'll pay for it."

"With what money dear," mom asks.

"My school money," I respond.

There's a pause and both parents object. "You earned that for school. Don't worry about it. We will handle it."

"No," I respond. "I want to do this." Tears are starting to swell up., but I hold them off.

"Cece," Mom says using my nickname, "we won't let you."

"We'll take care of it, but thank you," dad says.

"It's my money," I respond. My voice trembles some. "I love Gene too. I'm not going to stand by and let you do more hours on the job so you can help pay for medical bills." I wipe a few tears away. Mom embraces me and starts to cry. "I love this family too, I wanna' help, I wanna' help." My dad embraces me and we all stand there in the visitor room sobbing. I look over at ocean who's wiping her own eyes and motion for her to come over.

The next day is good. Gene is recovering. He will have some concussion like symptoms but is better. The doctors where able to implant some of his teeth, but had to use fake ones in other areas. We talk with him and he's in good spirits. That's excellent.

Without hesitation, I give mom and dad the money I raised. I am serious. There was no waver in my mind. They thank me and still try to change my mind. Not happening.

Later that day we hear a knock at the door. Mom answers it and sees someone she doesn't know. I hear her interact with the person and eventually let him in. I'm on the laptop but not really paying attention to what's in front of me until she calls my name.

"Coming," I respond. Strange but I head downstairs to see a youthful looking man but one who's clearly at least my mother's age. There were some grey spots in his goatee, which gave his age away. Then again, he might be graying early.

"Hello," he says with a clear voice.

"Hi," I respond. We shake hands.

"You don't know me, but I've been asked to give you this." He hands me a white envelope that was sealed. Mom's face is full of excitement with her hands clasp together in anticipation.

"Okay," I say. I take the envelope and open it up. A check is there and I pull it out to see the most money my eyes have seen. Speechless.

"I believe that should cover your tuition for the next four years," the man says.

Still speechless. Mom bumps me and I snap out of staring at the check. "Yes," I say weakly. "Yes it will."

"Good."

"Thank you," I say. "Thank you so much." I hug the man, much to his surprise.

"Not a problem," he responds

We release and I look at the check again. "Who are you? What's your name?"

"Not important. But you have people who care about you." With that, he grins at us both and walks out the door into his luxury convertible car.

"Hillary," mom asks. Her family is rich. I bet it was her.

I was able to get Hillary and Ocean on Facebook. I had great news to tell them and thank Hillary for sending someone to help me. That was incredible and quite surprising. Both of them shows up at the Martin's Ice Cream Shoppe and can see the excitement in my face. We all order sundaes and sit in our favorite seats.

"What's the news," Ocean asks.

"Something great just happened to me," I respond. "I was there in my room on Facebook as usual right." Both of them nod. "And then came a stranger at the door. We talked briefly and he handed me a check to pay for my schooling for the next four years."

"Wow," Hillary says. "You didn't know who he was."

"Nope."

"Strange," Ocean says.

"True, but he said I had really good friends." With that, I look in Hillary's direction. She has to realize that I know the jig is up.

"What are you looking at me for?"

"You didn't send the guy over?"

"No, but that's weird that a stranger would do that." I glance in Ocean's direction and she's looking away from the both of us. "Ocean," I ask.

I can tell she doesn't want to say anything but I know the truth. "Well," she starts.

"I didn't know you had..."

"Not me, but I have an uncle. Jack."

"Why is that familiar," Hillary asks.

"The adventure guy," I say. "The one who goes all over the world?"

"Yeap. He's barely here in town so I figured you wouldn't know who he was."

"Wow," I start. "Thank you." My voice almost quivers but I regain composure.

"Please not that again," Ocean says with a grin. "I'm all cried out after last night."

"Of course, you knew I was going to give away all that I had for Gene," I respond. Hillary wouldn't have known in time. She learned about Gene's accident through text messaging but not the details of me giving the money away. Ocean was there the entire time and knew of a way she could help.

"Thanks," I say to her and look at Hillary as well. "Both of you mean so much to me."

"Just remember to come to my games if you can," Ocean says.

"Wouldn't miss it," I respond.

When life is at its lowest moment, God provides a means that is best for the situation.

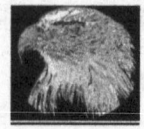

THE VOICE WITHIN

I Samuel 3:1-18

"Sam you almost ready," my mother yells.

"Yes ma'am," I respond. I fix my tie and check the teeth once more in the mirror. We're getting ready for worship. Our church, Victory Praise Temple, is under new leadership. Pastor Tyrone Williams has energized the church in the past six months. He immediately came in and revitalized the youth program. The former pastor was great but retired. Victory went through a few months with no true leadership until Pastor Tyrone came in.

The strangest thing is that everyone calls him Pastor Tyrone. Most of the time you call ministers and pastors by their last name; for some reason Pastor Tyrone prefers it the other way and no one cares. Being in middle school, that's cool with me. I like the guy so I don't mind getting ready for church.

"Sam," mom calls again.

"I'm ready," I answer back. I stop grooming myself and leave the bathroom. Mom gives me a look over while dad stands by the door. All of us had some kind of blue in our outfit. Mom loves to do this. Her goal is to get the family to look similar. She does it more often with her and dad, but she likes to include me as well.

She nods in approval and we all head for the car. The drive over is only about twenty minutes, or at least that's what dad says. I don't pay much attention. Too busy looking at my portable video game. Mom is actually cool about that, because she knows I'll pay attention in church.

I know mom loves me, but I think that sometimes she likes to smother. It has to be because I'm her only son. She loves to tell the story of how hard she prayed. Apparently mom was barren. She never had a miscarriage, but for some reason my parents could not have a child. That was until I came along. My miracle birth touched her so much that she named me Samuel, although everyone calls me Sam.

Church service starts as normal with the various preliminaries. During the service, a summer camp is mentioned. They bring some kids who went last year and random other youth. I'm barely interested but mom's large smile clearly tells me she's listening. That's weird, because I can't imagine her letting me go. Then again, to her, she has to learn how to trust in the Lord and let me be on my own. Granted, I'm not interested.

"What did you think about that summer camp," mom asks.

We're on our way back home. I stop playing the game and look towards the back of her seat. "It seems okay," I mumble.

"It sounds like fun, don't you think dear?"

"Yeah, sure," dad responds. He wasn't paying attention. She could ask him if the road would look better if it was painted pink for breast cancer and he would say, 'yeah, sure'.

"See your father agrees," mom says.

"Oh," I start, "okay." I didn't know what to say after oh. I'm not trying to be disrespectful but I figure she'll forget. Hopefully. The rest of the car ride is about the summer camp and the brochures she was able to get. She talked with Pastor Tyrone. I guess they have some spots open and he was telling her how great it would be for me to go. I'm still not interested and luckily, dad moves the conversation to baseball. Out of all the sports baseball is the only one that mom likes and doesn't mind talking about. I was in the clear until it came up that baseball was one of the summer camp activities.

After we ate, I go outside to the courts and meet with some friends. Bill loves playing and I know he'll be over there soon. The basketball courts are close to my house so I ride my bike. There are four courts and one of them us middle school kids play on. The high school students and older adults tend to go for the better rims. That's cool. I figure to wait until it's my time to go on the better courts.

When I arrive, shock and amazement floods my body as only three people where on the four courts. I'm shock more people where not out there but two of the people where playing H-O-R-S-E while another was on the court by herself. I recognize the solo player and walk in her direction.

"Marsha," I call out. She looks my way and smile. Marsha takes one more shot, collects the make, dribbles, and waits for me to come over.

"What's up Sam," she responds. Marsha is wearing her normal t-shirt and shorts. She has sort of this tomboyish look but feminine as well. It's hard to explain but the dimples in her face make her look cute.

"Meetin' Bill to shoot some hoops. Where is everyone?"

"There's a party for the high school students. I can't remember who's planning it, but you know they do this periodically. It's their way of getting the two schools together."

I forget that Brent and Wedgwood, fierce enemies in sports, come together on the beach and party. Makes sense. It's almost like a respectful rivalry. After all, we live in the same town, so we have to. Marsha and I go to the same middle school, Hubert, which is great. I'm not sure if we're scheduled to go to the same high school. I don't think we are, but who knows.

"What's new with you," I ask. We start shooting taking turns practicing jump shots. She's better at the game then I am. Make sense because she plays for the team. Me, I just play for fun. Bill and I both play for fun, nothing serious like the school team.

"Getting my jump shots together," Marsha responds. "Now that Cecilia and Ocean are gone, I'm the lead on the team."

"Oh yeah, they're going on to do big things in high school."

"Exactly," Marsha says. I pause for a minute and my mind drifts. Marsha stops shooting and laughs. "You thinking about Cecilia?"

"What?"

"I can tell by your face. You should say something to her. She goes to your church," Marsha says.

"I know, but then I get speechless. Can't talk. Mind gets crazy."

"I see," Marsha says and swishes a three pointer. She shakes her head and catches the pass I give her. "I don't get it, she's nice, but guys really love Cecilia."

Marsha is a girl, so there's no way I'm going to go in details on Cecilia's looks. It's not that she's more developed then others. Ocean and her other friend, Hillary, are pretty much the same. It's just that Cecilia got something different about her. Her eyes are warm in color and looks while her hair flows like a constant fan is blowing it.

I look at Marsha and shrug my shoulders. "I don't know. She's cute."

"Whatever," Marsha responds and swishes another three.

From a distance, we can see a pudgy guy on a bike. It's Bill. Marsha sighs. "What you doing for the summer," she asks. The other two on the court finishes their game of HORSE.

"I don't know, mom wants me to go to summer camp. I don't feel like it."

"You should go; it's not as bad as you think."

"Really?"

"Yeah, I would, but my family is going to Colorado for awhile."

I nod with genuine surprise. "That's cool," I respond. "Never been."

"It's lovely. Have family out there. I'll probably work on cooking at high altitudes plus work on stamina. Thin air really helps with conditioning."

"You're serious," I ask. Bill is closer and Marsha looks in his direction then at me. "About basketball."

"Yeap. Hey I'm about to take off. See you around."

"Okay."

Bill parks his bike near Marsha's and mine. He's gets near her and I could tell that he sniffs the air. Marsh sees him and shakes her head. They said hi and she was gone with her basketball. Bill jogs over to me and looks around at the court. The first two people playing HORSE included a third person. They start a new game and the last guy isn't that good.

"Where is everybody," he says in a raspy voice. Bill must be going through those changes they keep telling us about in school where it drops and squeaks. Strange. I guess my voice crack sometimes, which is peculiar.

"Beach party."

"Oh yeah, I forgot." Bill looks in Marsha's direction as she heads home and then at me. "She's pretty."

"Who, Marsha?"

"Yeah, aren't you best friends?"

"We've known each other for awhile, yeah," I respond.

"Kiss her?"

"No, why do you want to know?"

Bill shrugs. "She smells good."

"I saw you sniff the air around her, kind of weird," I respond.

"Can't help it, she makes me feel funny. Gotta sniff the air. Hey guess what?"

I look around. Notice that neither of us have a ball. I'm so use to others bringing theirs that I didn't even think to grab my own. Bill is waiting for me to respond and I shrug my shoulders.

"I'm going to this summer camp, that mom signed me up for."

"Really?"

"Yeah, it's going to be great. They have camping, nature, baseball, and all kind of other stuff. You should come. I think there are some rooms left."

"I don't know, not into camps, you know."

"Not really," Bill responds. "I'm just sayin' it'll be fun."

I look at Bill then at the court we're standing on. I could play basketball and video games but why not change it up. What plans do I have? It's not as if we're going on a vacation. I think we're going to Aruba for Christmas, which sounds great. Our family has other plans but I can't remember them. Bill stares at me. He's waiting for an answer. Hmm, what should I do?

****

Mom cries as she and dad drops me off at camp. They're going to miss me. I'm sure of it. She's surprised that I changed my mind on going to camp. After talking with Bill and somewhat Marsha, I change my mind. It might be fun, and I can make the best of it.

"You have to let me go mom," I say. Mom gives me one more squeeze and then pulls away.

"C'mon dear," dad begins, "he'll be fine." He wraps his arm around her. Mom smiles. They walk to the car, dad with a little more pep in his step compare to moms. That's cool I expect that.

"Glad to see you came," Bill says with that same raspy voice. He scratches his side as he walks toward me.

"I told you I was coming."

"Oh yeah, right after we saw Marsha on the courts."

I shake my head and walk inside the cabin I will stay in for the next week. Each cabin is large enough for eight boys. I should say eight campers since I image that the girls have their own on a different side of the camp.

The cabin has two sides divided by a large wall. Each side fits four beds. At the end of the cabin is a bathroom large enough for three guys to shower in their separate stall. There are toilets, and spaces to put a minimum amount of toiletries. The other end of the cabin is the counselor's room in charge of the sleeping quarters.

Bill and I get there at a decent time so we choose our beds right next to each other and near the bathroom. This way we can get in early for a quick shower or if we need to use the bathroom.

The camp gave us some time to see the area and get use to it. That was fun as Bill and I explore the campsite. We even meet our house counselor. His name is Elliot and he's from a town almost a hundred miles away. Apparently, he's a teacher and loves working at the camp because of his own camp experience and love for children. Elliot seems young so he's probably not that far out of college. Bill and I didn't learn much of his life but want to explore the place.

There is plenty of rolling hills, trees to climb, various ponds to fish, pools to swim, and a sports area for fun. There are a few basketball courts, sand volleyball, swimming, slides, and of course the baseball diamond. Bill and I meet up with some other guys who live 10 miles away from Sheridan Falls. They where talking about playing in the weekly baseball game that the camp put cabin mates against one another. Bill and I take their word for it since neither of us has ever been here before.

"This is going to be great," Bill says as we walk away from the guys.

I take in the sun, nice breeze, and nod. "Yeap."

We meet Elliot officially with the six other cabin mates about an hour later. He talks about the background of the camp, rules, and various other things. Most of us nod our heads and pay little attention. I'm sure Elliot is use to this reaction. In his mind, he knows that we will ask questions later as well as break a few rules.

Later we eat and play basketball until night. Then there is an assembly of some sort in the main hall. This camp is sponsored by various churches throughout the region so there are some religious activities planned.

"I thought we'll get a break from this," Bill whispers.

I chuckle and shake my head. "You signed up through a church didn't you."

"I don't know," Bill starts, "mom did it for me."

After the program, we go back to the cabin and chill. As cabin mates we got to know each other and learn where everyone is from. Bill and I wasn't the only two who came in with a friend. Four guys all came in together and slept on the other side of the room. The two on our side didn't know anyone but was cool. All they talk about is baseball, so I hope that translates to playing on the diamond when the baseball games happen.

At night, there were some faint noises from the cabin next to us. It was strange, almost like chanting or singing. I couldn't tell because of the distance. Elliot got up from his room and came into our side of the cabin then the other. I can tell he wants to see if we're causing all the trouble.

"Be right back," Elliot says. He leaves and I can tell by the mumbling that another counselor came out to meet him.

"You think someone is getting their praise on," Bill whispers.

The two guys on our side laugh and we all go silent when we think Elliot is coming back. It wasn't him so I say, "Who knows. Maybe the service really got to them."

"Or they could be…" before Bill's and I roommates finish, we hear yelling and slamming of the doors.

I can't tell what's going on, but clearly, the guys in the cabin near us got in trouble. Bill was trying to tell a joke, but I hush him so I can hear what is going on. Only traces were coming through. One of the guys from the other side of the cabin came over. He wants to know what is going on.

"Someone got in trouble from next door," I respond.

"We just got here," the boy from the other side says. "What could they do to get in trouble?"

I shrug my shoulders and press towards the windows in hopes of seeing something. The guys are being lead out by a group of counselors and in the direction of the administration building. "I hear babbling or something," I say.

"Drugs," Bill suggests.

"Could be," one of the guys says.

"They're headed towards the administration building."

"I've seen that before," the guy from the other side of the cabin says. "They're probably being kicked out. So it was serious."

"Elliot is coming," I say in a loud whisper. Everyone goes to their beds as though nothing happen. We try to fake sleep but Elliot knows better.

"Good night guys. See you in the morning."

The next day, the entire camp was a buzz as to what happened in the cabin next to us. All eight guys where kicked out, and the cabin locked. Curiosity is too strong for most as we ask our counselors what happened. They didn't go into detail, but inform us to obey the rules and remind us that this is a Christian camp. That doesn't mean that everything is God and Jesus all the time but there are some values they want to instill.

During the middle of the day Bill and I sit near one of the pools. The girls are having fun swimming while the guys try their best to dunk one another. Others are around the pools soaking in the sun.

"This is cool," Bill says.

"Yeap."

"These girls are nice, not Marsha nice, but nice."

"Why do you keep bringing her up all the time," I ask.

One of the guys splashes some of the girls standing near the side of the pool who didn't want to get wet. "I dunno', she's pretty and likes sports. You don't feel something when you're near her."

"Never looked at her like that."

"You should. She smells great," Bill says.

"I know, I see you inhale the air around her every time she's near." We both laugh. Bill looks in the direction past the trees at our cabins.

"What do you think happen?"

"I don't know. Strange."

Elliot is watching the kids at the pool. It must be his turn as the lifeguard and make sure no one is injured. There's a slight edge with all the campers, but that has to be expected with the events from last night.

"Was he the lifeguard yesterday when we got here," I ask Bill.

"Who?"

"Elliot," I say. Bill pause for a moment but he has no idea who I'm talking about. "Our cabin counselor."

"Oh yeah, him. I don't know," Bill responds. "Keep thinking about that cabin."

More random yelling and screaming from the girls who didn't want to get wet are now in the pool having fun with the guys. Elliot looks bored but stares at the kids. He's really into his job. Then again, can't blame him. Whatever happened last night probably messed with his mind.

"What if we sneak in," Bill suggests.

"What?"

"Tonight, we sneak in."

I look at Bill. He can tell I'm not amused with his suggestion. "Is this one of your jokes?"

"Nope. All serious."

"Bill, that's stupid. So we can get kicked out. Think about it," I say. Bill nods. He looks in the direction of our cabins.

"Okay."

"Okay what?"

"I'll think about it," Bill responds.

"Really, you're going to break into that cabin? They probably cleaned it up by now," I whisper.

Bill looks at me and smile. "True, but it still sounds fun. I won't go tonight. But I'll think about it."

"Okay, let's shoot some hoops." We leave the area and Elliot is checking two girls to make sure they're okay. I didn't see what happen but I guess he's making sure that they're not injured. He takes them away from the pool and I guess to the medic or staff.

That night the cabin next door is constantly in my head. What was the babbling and yelling? For some reason I can't understand what was going on. Bill assumes that it was drugs. Maybe. After all, we cannot have drugs and use them on the campgrounds. Especially not on a place that is having religious services at night and imparting a Christian background into the youth. News of drugs would hurt the face of this camp and destroy the reputation.

It's nighttime and I'm fast asleep. It takes awhile but I get Bill to forget about going into the abandoned cabin. "Sam," a voice calls. I wake up and look around. Bill looks like he's asleep plus his voice is raspy. This was calm. Almost soothing. The other two guys don't need me, so I go to Bill's bed and wake him up.

"What's up?"

Bill looks around confused. "What."

"You called me."

"No, no I didn't."

That makes sense. His voice is raspy. This voice was calm. Almost soothing. Is it possible that Elliot called me? How could no one else hear him? I know I'm not crazy. It wasn't a dream and someone called me. I leave Bill's bedside and head towards Elliott room.

"Elliott," I say and knock on his door. Elliott comes to the door a little disheveled. "Sam, you okay?"

"Yeah, you called."

Elliott looks around and then at me. "What?"

"I heard my name, did you call me?"

Another pause. "No," Elliott responds. "Probably a dream."

"Yeah," I say, "sorry."

Elliott nods and I go back to bed. Strange I thought for sure I heard a voice but go to sleep. Within a few minutes, I hear the same thing.

"Sam."

I wake up and look at Bill. He's snoring. The other two guys are out as well. It has to be Elliott. I sigh and run quietly to Elliott's door and knock. The cabin counselor answers the door and he's clearly not happy.

"Is this a joke, you okay?"

"Yeah," I respond. "I definitely heard you calling my name. "

Elliott stares at me and then pushes me slightly out the way and peer into the room. All the guys are there and asleep. He looks at me again.

"See," I start, "they're all asleep."

"You heard a voice."

"Yes."

"Well, try to get some sleep. I saw you where out in the sun. Maybe it's affecting you."

"How where those girls," I ask.

"What?"

"The girls. Before Bill and I left, you where helping them or something."

"They're fine. Perfect. Now go to bed," Elliott says.

I go back to bed and figure he's right. It was hot. Sometimes heat does crazy things to you. I blow out a few breaths and try to relax. The night is quiet and my eyes open. I'm waiting for the voice. Nothing. Elliott was right. My eyes shut and I relax into the pillow.

"Sam," the voice says again.

I didn't even fall asleep, so I know I'm hearing it. This time I go to Elliott. I'm surprise that the other three did not wake up. Elliott doesn't even look sleepy when he answers the door again. Instead of annoyance, he studies my face. He can tell I'm serious.

"The next time you hear the voice respond, speak Lord, for your servant is listening."

Now I pause. Didn't expect that. I had to say it in my head again to make sure that I hear him right. Elliott can tell that I understood what he said and nod. I shrug, smile and lay down again. No way, it's God speaking to me that clearly. I try to stay up. For some reason the idea of God talking sounds weird. I'm not anyone special, just a young guy at summer camp. Eventually, I fall asleep and hear it again.

"Sam."

There's slight hesitation but I respond. "Speak Lord, for your servant is listening."

"I need for you to deliver a message to Elliott."

Air almost leaps from my body. There's no way I thought that would happen. I read stuff like this in The Bible, but those where prophets and special people who talk with God. Honesty, I thought that was a euphemism. Why me? Who am I? I'm no one. In spite of that. There's no way I can ignore that. Who ignores God?

I go to Elliott and he shows up to the door with a grin. "So I was right," Elliott says.

"Yes."

"What did He say?" I knew the message but didn't want to say. "Go on."

I tell Elliott what God wants me to say. It was personal. Elliott knows where he has to make changes in his life. He's always known. To have your thoughts confirmed by a soon to be eighth grader is overwhelming.

For some reason, after that night, I didn't care what happened in the cabin. Hearing a message like that was surreal. I never thought of myself as a mouthpiece for God. Elliott and I kept the conversation between us. No one needed to know. That was for Elliott from God. No one, not even me, needed to dwell on the topic and the voice within my head that night. No one.

Listen when God communicates with you.

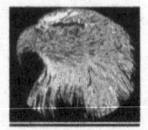

INTUITION

Luke 2:40-50

"Hi, the name's Jack. Jack Colt."

"Is that necessary," Aaron says. I laugh because I love saying my name as though I'm a secret agent. Can't help myself. I watch all the Bond movies and read the books. It's the adventure. Even the "Mission Impossible" films and "A-Team" shows are some of my favorite programming.

"Sorry Cuz'," I respond. I'm not saying that to be randomly friendly but he's my actual cousin. Our mothers are sisters and we have been raised as brothers for most of our lives. The amazing thing is that we're opposite. I like adventure; he prefers resting in a peaceful place. I'm a roller coaster fanatic he rides carousels. My cars are fast, big, and pure gas-guzzlers. His are small hybrids. This is why I'm shocked he even came on this trip.

We are currently in the tourist city of Sleipnir in the middle of winter to get ourselves acclimated to climbing Mount Cadeyrn. Granted, it's a volcano but I figure to climb it before it explodes and covers the northwest in ash, lava, and dirt. The site from Sleipnir is amazing and with each passing day, I get excited. Can't wait to climb a mountain knowing there's that much power underneath.

Sleipnir sits at the base of Cadeyrn. There's another mountain behind Cadeyrn called Colelinger. I'm not exactly sure as to why they're called that but Sleipnir derives its name from Norse mythology. According to mythology, Sleipnir is the name of a fast horse that has eight legs. You see random pictures, posters, and a few statues of this eight-legged beast. This little tourist town has used its name and main attraction, Mount Cadeyrn as a means to support itself. Usually most tourist arrive spring through autumn. No one climbs during the winter for two reasons, horrible weather and possible avalanches. This is why I want to climb now. It's going to be great conquering this mountain during the wintertime.

There are six of us and we're thrilled to be climbing Cadeyrn. Well, save for Aaron. He came because I promised he could bring his camera and film us on this expedition. The one thing my cousin loves is filmmaking and travel videos. This is by far the most adventurous trip he's ever done.

"This is for the launch of the site," Aaron says.

Right now, he's starting up his own online travel channel video. He did some local parks around Sheridan Falls and it got some decent hits. Then I told Aaron about Tom and me bringing our wives to climb Mount Cadeyrn. Aaron had the idea that this would boost his hits. For some reason he wants to make me the lead for the video. I'm cool with that. Don't mind being the star.

"I have to be me," I say. "After all the audience will be in for a treat. Climbing an active volcano is going to be..."

"Active," Aaron says. His voice echoes through my room. Each of the couples got their own room including Aaron and his current girlfriend. Maybe not girlfriend, they've only been dating, and I mean loosely dating, for about six weeks. She is a major fan of rock climbing so she had no problem coming with Aaron on this trip.

Aaron is in my room so I can set a background on this trip for his film. I didn't mean to mention the active part. I forgot that Aaron assumed that it's dormant. This is true, for the most part.

"I didn't mean active, like lava is pouring out."

"Oh."

"We couldn't climb it then, but I assure you its safe. Glad the weather is holding up."

Aaron nods. He pulls his camera out and points it on me. "For real this time."

I roll my eyes, clear the throat, and stand next to the window. "Hi I'm Jack Colt and today, we're climbing Mount Cadeyrn. It's the middle of winter yet the weather looks good. So we're not afraid."

"Weather people say they're might be a snowstorm," Aaron says from behind the camera.

"They've said that for the past three days. That's why we've been sitting here wasting time in Sleipnir instead of enjoying ourselves on the mountain. Besides its elements, we'll be fine."

Aaron pauses for a moment. He's nervous. He's really hoping for no weather issues, I'm not worried. Aaron turns the camera off right before I was about to introduce the climbing team.

"Hey what you're doing," I ask. "I was about to introduce everyone on the team."

"Without their faces," Aaron asks. "We would have to do it all over again."

I silently agree. Aaron looks at the camera and then sets something on the focus. He points it at me again and we talk a little about Mount Cadeyrn, the mountain range we're in and even Sleipnir. It is the information to have as background for his online video.

Thirty minutes later, all six of us are eating a buffet breakfast in Grand Sleipnir Hotel. This is the tallest and grandest building in the city with eight floors. Each level is because of the eight legs of the horse the city is named after. The bottom floor is by far the largest with a restaurant and buffet area. There are several meeting rooms, a lounge where live music is played during the summer and a few pools available during spring and summer. The entire hotel is decorated with a Maroon and Gold trim. It gives the place a sort of elegance and traditional class.

During breakfast, we talk about past personal adventures and the future of climbing this mountain. It's cold. A little unusually cold for this season but that makes it fun. I've climbed Mount Kilimanjaro and Kosciuszko. Surfed in the Atlantic and Pacific Oceans. Skydived on three continents, skied on four, and swam with whales, rays, and sharks. Next on my list is to climb the largest island mountain called Puncak Jaya in New Guinea.

While we are talking, an older gentleman strolls up to the table. His beard and hair is silver. He has the eyes of a seasoned man who has seen danger and survived. His wrinkles need moisture while his toothless grin peers behind thin lips. We assume he's going to say something. The table is quiet.

"You goin' up on Cadeyrn," the man asks.

"Yeah," I respond. "Ever been?"

"Once" he says holding a single finger in the air. It shakes a little and he places it next to his side.

"Any pointers," I ask. The rest of the table wish I will stop talking to the old guy. I can tell by their loud sighs. They're annoyed with his presence and probably me.

"Don't go."

"That scary," I ask with a laugh.

"During this season," the man responds. "Winter is never good. Not safe."

"Because of the snow," Aaron asks. There is uneasiness in his voice. I can tell my cousin is nervous.

"We'll be fine," I say.

"A storm is brewing," the man says.

"I checked the forecast, its okay," I say.

"You also have avalanches and the Volnaco," the old man states.

"Avalanches are rare on this mountain and you mean Volcano. Cadeyrn has been dormant for a century. We're fine," I argue.

The old man pauses and stops rocking back and forth. "I didn't say Volcano," the man says. He looks around the room that is only a fourth full and then back into my eyes. "I said the Volnaco."

"Volnaco," Suzie, my wife starts. "What's that?"

"That is the name of those who partake in the forbidden flesh. This tribe has built their appetites for the greatest of all hunters. The Volnaco are the fable eaters of men and in the winter they live on Cadeyrn."

"Cannibals," I ask. "Please tell me you're joking."

"I'm not joking," the old man responds.

"I'm curious," Thomas, my friend, starts. "Who are the Volnaco?"

"Seriously Thomas," I say.

"Let him finish" Suzie says.

"From spring to autumn, Cadeyrn is available to the public and tourist. You may climb to your heart's desire. But in winter, the Volnaco uses the mountain as a hiding place from the harsh elements."

"They go to a mountain to get away from the weather," I say aloud so my friends can hear how crazy that sounds.

"About fifty miles from here they live in a planes-like area. Its flat area is good for the warm season but brutal in winter."

"See Jack," Suzie says. "Continue."

"So during the winter, the Volnaco comes to Cadeyrn to hide in the caves on the opposite side of the mountain. They go there for protection and mating."

"This is ridiculous," I mumble.

The old man stares at me and grins," Don't go, unless you have a desire to be next on the menu."

I look to the side and a few hotel officers spot the old man. He begins to walk away knowing that he is caught. "If you want to stay alive, stay off the mountain." The old man runs out the room with the hotel staff following after.

"Let's go," I say.

We finish eating, check out, and then make our way to Cadeyrn. It's definitely cold and the temperature is dropping. We all plan for this and have plenty of clothes and protection suits. There was little talk about the old man and people on the mountain. Suzie thought it was a cute little tale. Aaron is a little concerned; he has no plans to make a low budget horror film. I agree. It's at the base where Aaron whips out the camera and wants me to introduce everyone.

"Greetings, you already know me, Jack Colt. I'm joined by my wife Suzie."

"Hi," Suzie says and waves at the camera. We've been together for years. Like me, she loves adventure and is from Sheridan Falls.

"My good friend, Dr. Thomas Spitz."

"Tom is fine," he says. Tom is a professor at Sheridan State University. He loves culture and has tender in the history department. Tom travels the world to find cultures and learn more about society.

I chuckle and point towards the woman next to him, "that's his wife Karen." She waves and gets closer to Tom. Karen loves Tom. She goes with him when she can. She loves skiing and is a little upset that she can't ski on this mountain.

"Over here we have Liz Hampton but she's not alone and came with the cameraman and producer of this project Aaron Trudeau." Aaron gives me the thumbs up and smiles. "Behind us is Mount Cadeyrn. We will climb and conquer."

The group cheers and Aaron soaks it in. He's truly excited and thrilled. Because not all of us are expert climbers there's no way we can make it to the summit. I would love too but it's too risky. I'm a thrill seeker not suicidal. Despite that, we still had to register with the ranger station. They strongly didn't want us to go up. Their reason was the changing weather. Aaron is hoping that's the only reason.

We go up and start the climb. It's rougher then I expect but fun. On the way up Aaron is getting some great shots filming nature and us climbing. It's a lot of snow and rock, but it still looks great. Especially the views of the surrounding areas. From a distance, we see what looks like a dark cloud.

"Think that's a problem," Suzie asks.

"Hopefully not," I whisper.

The rest of the group pays attention to the mass but don't think anything about it. Its two hours later when the cloud is actually a rolling storm heading for us. From a distance, it does not look big but now I realize the storm the old man was talking about is heading right for us. I thought for sure the weatherman stated that we where going to have good conditions. We where too far up to make it down in time. Its okay we prepared for this.

Before the storm comes, we set up a strong tent to protect us from the elements. We know it can be a little crazy but figure to be okay. We plan to spend the night on the mountain to ride out the storm, to reach a certain point and then return down.

The storm comes in with fury. The wind is howling and the snow is falling fast. To be honest I assume this would be a small flurry but this is much worst. Aaron gets some shots outside the tent and pulls the camera back inside. The new storm drops the temperature. We are all thankful for snow suites.

The clouds are so thick that it covers the landscape like night. The tent rattles but we hold it still. Aaron is close to Liz with a slight smile on his face. Think she likes him. I was joking earlier about their relationship but she wouldn't come this far with some guy she barely knew even if she does like climbing.

"This is fun," Liz says. Her voice is unreal. It's very high and pitchy. Still she has a great smile, while her teeth chatter.

"Yeah," Tom says. "Never been through anything like this before."

"Tell me about it, this storm is..." before I finish there's a rumble.

"Thunder," Aaron asks.

I shake my head. The group is silent as we wait. There's some wind and more snow.

"I guess it pass..." Suzie starts and then it rumbles again.

We brace ourselves and look around. The wind of the storm is now competing with the rumble of the ground and a distant roar coming towards us.

"Earthquake," Karen yells.

"No," I shout. I stick my head out the tent and walk out protecting my face from the whipping snow. I look through my snow goggles and am shock at how dark it is. Some sun is still peaking through and in a distance; I see a wave in the air. There's no way it could be a tornado. I stare. Then it dawns on me.

Immediately I run into the tent. "Avalanche," I scream.

The group looks around. Stun with disbelief. They come out the tent almost shoving each other. The rumble is getting closer and the snow continues to push our way. Aaron never lets go of his camera and I can't see his eyes through the snow goggles but I bet they're large from fear.

Some of us grab some supplies but we try to rush down the mountainside. In reality, we probably should stay in the tent but fear takes over. The avalanche comes roaring at us and it will not be stop. I did not realize that it could be this bad while a storm is pouring snow.

Some of the rumble was from below. The avalanche is so strong that it causes the ground to shake. The roaring of the avalanche comes closer. It is as if the mountain wants us off and it's trying to accomplish that feat.

There's a pause in everyone's movement. We look around and see the imminent rushing snow, mud, and mountain come at us. There's a realization that there's no way we can race down this mountain and out run it. We've been running and the tent is a mere fifty meters away. My chest thumps. I'm tired and the avalanche is heading for us.

"Maybe if we come together," someone shouts. I think it was female but the howling wind makes it hard to decipher. We all hear it and band together. I'm not sure if this will work, but maybe as a group, we would be heavier and be able to withstand nature's fury.

A small prayer comes out of my mouth. The rumbles are closer. I pray a little harder, I think most of us do. Right before it happens there was almost a moment of silence. It wasn't real silence more like a peace. It's going to be okay.

The rush of snow, mud, and pieces of rock roared through as though we aren't huddle together. The force was so strong that it broke our group up immediately upon impact. The calm moment I had left and panic took over. Now I'm a part of the roar and so is everyone I imagine. The constant barrage of snow falling is small compare to the avalanche.

I try to swim against the current but that doesn't work. It almost seems to have a mind or character of its own. It carries us down the mountain with such ease. There is a loud thumping noise from a distance.

My snow goggles are still on which is amazing. I look around and peer through the snow falling from the sky and surrounding me like a giant pool. In the distance is a huge boulder that is being flung around by Cadeyrn's force.

I'm nervous and try to get out of its way. The boulder has to be the size of a pickup truck or possibly bigger and it goes with the snow as well as bounces in the air a little. The boulder hits the ground often, which causes it to jump in the air. I try to scream and move at the same time. It's no use. The mountain has me and the boulder is getting closer. I muffle out "Jesus," as the boulder continues its path. My lips are cold but that's not my concern.

The boulder is larger then I expected as it proceeds to get closer. It's the size of a semi truck cab and it is tumbling towards me. There's a loud bang and the boulder hits something on the mountain and flips over and to the side of me.

It hits the side of the mountain only five yards to my left and the impact pushes me away and into the snow. I look around for the others but really can't find anyone. It's dark, snowy and the avalanche is overwhelming. I think there's a faint yell but don't see anything.

As sudden as it starts the avalanche ceases. It must of reach a resting point, which is great for me. The most unbelievable thing is that I'm still on top of the snow. Most people are buried in a situation like this but here I am partially covered and on top.

It's a struggle to get up but I force myself too so the falling snow won't bury me. I'm sore and in pain. Nothing is broken or not working. All limbs work. I'm pressing through on top of the snow looking around. I can't see anyone. The boulder is visible but none of my companions.

Please don't tell me I lead everyone up here to die. Please don't tell me that. I can't live with myself. Don't let my wife, cousin, best friend, and their companions die. Please Lord. Please.

I take one more step and fall to the snow. The falling drops of frozen water seem to be lessening. I look up and there is an impeding break in the storm. That's great. Whew. Too tired to move. Can't rest. It's too cold. I'm so sore. Have to keep moving. Have to keep….

There's a small tap on my face and I wake up. A little boy is standing above me, smiling. He's dressed in some think animal skin coat. The sun is bright and shines all around him. It's almost angelic, but the cold is a quick reminder that this isn't heaven.

I almost go back to sleep but he puts something under my nose. That wakes me up and immediately gets my body going. That was strong. It has to be smelling salt. I've seen that used on football players to test them for concussion symptoms.

"Thank you," I say then look at the boy. He's clearly of Native American or Eskimo background. He probably doesn't know English; hopefully he can tell I'm grateful.

"You're welcome," the boy responds. He can tell by my response that I'm shock he knows English. "Don't be alarm, I know English," he says. That's a relief. Wait, he's not one of those Volnacos? Was the old man right? He was correct about the storm. I look into the young man's eyes hopefully he's wrong.

He stands up and surveys the snowy area. My friends. I get up too, but slower then him. The avalanche really took it out of me. I'm sore but alive. Thank God for that. The boy runs to my left and digs a little. In the distance, I see a bright red coat partially submerge like myself in the snow.

It's Karen. I help the young boy and we pull Karen out of the snow. She was only partially in so she's not dead or frozen but I'm sure very cold. He taps her face and she barely wakes up. Then like myself put some of the special smelling salt under her nose. Like me, she wakes up and is startled to see the young man next to me.

"Hot drink," he says, "over there." With that, the young man points behind me and I see a bag that is sitting on the snow. I'm sure there's something in it so I rush over and bring the bag. It's heavier then I expect but set it in front of the young man.

There are three bottles strap in a special animal skin or material. He allows Karen to drink and I can tell it's strong but warm. She shivers and her eyes widen with clarity. Whatever he gave her it did the trick.

She thanks the young boy and is surprise like myself that he can speak English. Sometimes you respond with what come natural even if you assume the other person has no idea what you're saying. I look over past the boy and Karen to see a few other bright color coats. He sees them too.

We rush to separate people and begin digging them out. It's great that no on is completely submerged in the snow. We are all cold but that special elixir the young man has is helping our bodies. The last person we found as a group was Aaron. He was next to the boulder and unconscious.

I hope the boulder didn't land on him. The little boy rush to Aaron's side and try the smelling salt trick. It works but Aaron is in great pain. I can tell by the way that he moves that his trip during the avalanche was not pleasant at all. The boy still gave Aaron some of the warming elixir and my cousin feels refresh but in pain.

The young man checks Aaron's legs. Nothing broken. That's a relief. It would be hard carrying him off this mountain. The route we took wasn't as bad, but there's no telling where the avalanche carried us. I'm not sure how to get down from where we are. The tent with some of the supplies and map could be anywhere.

"Shoulder," the young man says.

Aaron winces and nods his head. The young man reaches into the side of the pouch and has a cream as well as bandages. He is prepared for everything. Maybe he's done this before.

He gently presses the cream on Aaron shoulder after pulling back his coat. Aaron winches in pain and grits his teeth. He's staying strong while the rest of us look in amazement. I didn't know if it would heal immediately but I don't believe that was the point.

"It soothes and numbs pain," the boy says. He responded as though he could hear my thoughts. What am I thinking now? C'mon. He continues rubbing I guess he's not a mind reader. The snowstorm made me crazy.

The young man then takes a bandage and wraps it around Aaron. He does it gently but makes it secure so Aaron wouldn't move his arm to much. After he is done, he zips up Aaron's coat and stand.

"Thank you," Aaron says. We help him up and Liz looks at the young man.

"What's your name," Liz says slowly.

"Niyol," he responds quickly. I didn't think to ask for his name. Niyol responds so quickly I think he's trying to get us to realize that he knows English. Probably wants us to stop speaking to him as if he can't.

"Thank you Niyol," I say. This time I respond to him in a normal pace and sound. My hope is that everyone else will follow suit.

We look around. Niyol can tell that we have no idea how to get back. Each couple gets a little closer to their partners. Niyol doesn't panic and puts his supplies away.

"Follow me," Niyol says.

Some of us are a little hesitant. I'm sure they, like myself is thinking about the Volnaco. I start and wave everyone to follow.

There's not much choice in the matter. The avalanche carried us away from base camp and we don't know where we are going. I remember coming in a direction opposite of where Niyol is going but that doesn't matter. We had to of been out here for much of the day and maybe he knows a cave in the mountain. Doesn't the Volnaco live in caves? I hope the old man is wrong.

"How did you find us," Tom asks. We had been walking for only ten minutes. Mostly in silence, pain, shock, and some fear.

"Intuition."

"That's some intuition you got there," Suzie says. She wasn't being funny but genuinely surprise. We can understand if the rangers had found us. We had to check in with them, but some boy on the side of the mountain.

"I always listen to my intuition," Niyol responds. "It's never failed."

"Is that how you know where to go?"

"Yeap."

The group all look at one another. Should we be following a boy who could be no older then twelve to some unknown spot? My mind races to the old man. His story about the people who live on this mountain during the winter; I thought he was lying. Is it true?

"You live around here," I ask.

"Not too far."

"Oh," Liz responds. Her high-pitched voice pierces the air. I can't believe she's a teacher. That has to get on the students nerves. Then again, if she can relay the information in a clear way, who cares what she sounds like.

"You where lead in the right direction," Niyol says.

"Actually, I think our base is back the other way," Tom says. His voice shakes. He like everyone in the group keeps thinking the same thing about the Volnaco. Shame because Niyol probably wants to help.

"That's covered, we go this way. Trust me."

"How can we be sure," Tom asks. Sometimes his intelligence is annoying but he does have a point. Then again, if Niyol hadn't shown up, we would probably be ice cubes.

Niyol stops and faces Tom. He looks behind us and then at him. "If you want, you can go," Niyol says and point in the direction Tom suggests. There's silence between us. The wind stops. Great. The constant cold was annoying.

"Never mind," Tom says.

Niyol nods and then looks at us. "Anyone else?" We shake our heads. "Let's go then, its getting dark soon. Trust me," Niyol says, "intuition."

We follow Niyol as he continues walking. Some of the snow actually makes some of the trip easier. It's still rough climbing the paths but we manage. Aaron is able to stay with us even though it's tough. His girlfriend and I take turns holding his camera and filming different things. We made sure that Niyol is okay with being on camera. We assume that natives to the mountain might believe the camera stills his soul, but Niyol tells us he doesn't believe that.

Tom is convinced we're being taken to the Volnaco. He whispers his ideas and I know Niyol can hear him. During our walk, the young man gives Aaron some warm liquid to help him on the journey. Eventually Tom gets on Niyol's nerves and our guide stops the group.

"Listen," Niyol starts. "I've never heard of this Volnaco and there's no group around here who eat people. I know the old man who speaks such lies. He is a drunk and racist. I wouldn't listen to someone like that." Niyol looks at each of us and then continues walking. I give a quick glance to Tom and put my finger to my lips. Tom nods. He understands to be quiet for the rest of the walk.

After what seems like forever, Niyol leads us to a small ranger station and a few buildings around it. The avalanche must have pushed us pretty far down the hill or we didn't go up as far as we thought. A few rangers came out to meet us as well as an older woman to Niyol. We where wrong the entire trip. Niyol was leading us to safety. There were no stupid Volnaco as Niyol said. He was lead by his intuition.

The people check us and the woman is proud of her son. We thank Niyol and the rangers for their help and care. Aaron is very grateful that Niyol helped with his shoulder.

"I see you're out there listening to intuition again," the woman says to Niyol.

Our group, except for Aaron snaps our head around at the woman. That's some intuition.

"Excuse me," Suzie says, "did you say intuition?"

"Why yes," the woman responds. "Niyol always go out there whenever he feels like he should go and help someone."

"We don't know how he does it," the ranger says but he's great at doing that. "There where some other hikers and climbers out there and we found them, but Niyol packs his supplies and went out to find you."

"That's amazing that your intuition is so strong," Tom says, "I'm impressed."

"Not just mine," Niyol states. "But everyone's."

I look over at Niyol's mother. "What does he mean by that?"

"Intuition is how he relates. Every since he learned to navigate the mountain and the area from what he calls intuition."

"What do you call it," I ask her. There's something there. Something deeper.

"Jesus Christ, that's what all the villagers call the voice that leads our way."

Youth can show all people on how to trust God and listen to His words.

OBSIDIAN

Mark 9:2-29

Evil is real. I don't mean in the theoretical sense. I mean, real. I'm a minister. Wanted to be one every since I was in high school. My parents encouraged me because I was a good speaker. That's not the only requirement to being a pastor, but it helps. Never in my time as being a minister did I expect to confront evil. I know we call bad behaviors evil but there's a difference between bad habits and genuine evil. I didn't know that from the start of the ministry, but I know that now.

It was my first summer at Victory Praise Temple. I had graduated from school and was a minister at a smaller church for a few years before moving to Sheridan Falls. The former pastor of Victory Praise was a teacher of mine at the seminary. He knew me in school and was impressed with my studies and attentiveness in class. He also loved the fact that I had a passion for young people and believed they are the key to growing a church.

I had arrived at Victory early in spring. It was a little strange for the church members because the previous few ministers where at least in their fifties. I was in my upper twenties but the former minister made sure to bring me in and build a bond with the church board. After they saw some of my ideas work, then they came aboard. To be honest, it wasn't me, but praying to God for guidance. There was no way they where going to accept me without Him.

One of my main friends on the church board was Deacon Brown. He was a powerful figure on the board who listened to the previous pastor's advice on having me be the new minister. Just like the rest, Deacon Brown was skeptical, but took me in anyway. During the spring, Deacon Brown implored many of the board members to go with the ideas. Sometimes Deacon Brown would preach or lead out in various church services. He was the strongest member on the board but during the summer, he started to tail off.

Victory Praise went in with multiple churches around the region to send our young people to a summer camp. Deacon Brown was a big fan and proponent. He even sent his son. Then something happened and he stopped coming to church.

It was summer time so I figured it was a personal vacation but many people doubted that. Due to this, I plan a meeting with him at church. After about an hour of Deacon Brown not showing up, I talked with the church secretary.

"Where's Deacon Brown," I asked Rose, the church secretary. It was the middle of summer and the Victory Praise Temple was empty.

The only people there was myself, Rose, and a few people working or cleaning the church.

"He has home life issues," Rose responded. She seemed careful in telling me. It was as if she didn't want me to know but had to tell.

"Home life?"

"Yeah," she answered. "I'm not exactly sure what it is, but, it's something personal."

"So that's why he hasn't been to church. I set up a meeting with him today, hoping he would show," I said to Rose. I wasn't really looking for a response. Just speaking aloud and allowing the thoughts to circulate.

"Should you go see him," Rose asked. She said it more as a suggestion then a question. I understood her tone. She didn't want me to implicate her, but was concerned for Deacon Brown. I'm still not sure if she knew everything but had suspicions. At the time, it didn't matter. Deacon Brown needed help and I was going to provide it.

On the way to Deacon Brown's home, I called him. It took awhile but he answered the phone. We talked and I told him that the church was concerned. He was trying to give me the usual mess that everything was okay. I didn't believe it and told him that I was on the way. Deacon Brown was immediately nervous and didn't want me to come over. He insisted that we meet at a pizza place down the street from his house. I agreed and met him there soon after.

Deacon Brown was a tall man. The church picked him to be the head of the Deacon Board because of his physical size and relationship with the Lord. He's was usually clean-shaven and neat. When I saw him at the pizza parlor Deacon Brown wore a jersey with jeans and had face stubble.

"Deacon," I called out from the side of the pizza restaurant.

Deacon Brown walked over with shoulders slumped. He sat down next to me and sighed. "Pastor," he said with a slight country draw. His voice was similar to me like that of Scottie Pippen. Scottie always had a deliberate tone to his voice and pacing to his speech.

"How you been," I asked.

"Same," Deacon Brown started, "like I said on the phone."

"You're right; I didn't bring you here for small talk." A waitress came over and we ordered our pizzas and sodas. She left and I continued to talk with the Deacon. "I know something isn't right. You're not alone.

Whatever it is that you're going through, I'm not only here for you, but will help you through it."

"I doubt you can help me," Deacon Brown responded.

"You think I'm going to judge," I asked.

Deacon Brown thought for a while. "No."

"I promise I won't. I don't care if it's drinking, adultery," I said, then paused before my next response, "homosexuality."

"You think I'm gay," Deacon Brown asked but said that much quicker then everything else.

"No, but I'm not going to judge. I know people who can help with all things. Regardless."

Deacon Brown looked around. The waitress brought our sodas and smiled as she walked away. He took a sip and looked at me. "Not this one."

"You sure?"

"I'm not even sure what's going on."

"Try me," I responded.

Deacon Brown took another sip. He enjoyed diet clear sodas. This time I could tell it wasn't as good to him. He was thinking hard. His mind was mulling the situation.

"It's Pace," he responded.

"He went to the summer camp, right."

Deacon Brown grunted. "Yeah. Not for long."

"There where rumors," I said. "But I'm not into rumors or gossip. To me it doesn't get people or the situation any better."

"I see."

"Is he sick? I know allergies can be a mess."

"You can say that, yes. Sick."

He was hiding something but I couldn't tell if Pace got into something on purpose or by accident. I do remember that I had not seen Pace after the summer camp. Even before he wasn't active in church as he was when I first got to Victory Praise.

"Can I see him," I asked. "I have some anointing oil, and we can pray for his illness to leave."

Deacon Brown paused. A long pause. He was mulling it over. So it must have been a serious sickness. At the time, I assumed it was a little more serious then allergies. That didn't matter to me. Nothing is too hard for the Lord.

"Yes," Deacon Brown said. "But I don't want you to come over."

"I understand. Wherever you feel comfortable. The church is open and I can talk with Pace, see how he's doing, and we can pray for him. Then handle it according to God's will after that."

The waitress came over and placed the pizza on the table. She asked if we needed anything else and we asked for a few more napkins. Once she left we returned to our conversation.

"I should've come earlier," Deacon Brown said. He stared at one of his slices and blew on it to cool down.

"Sometimes we try to do things on our own. Especially if the situation is embarrassing. I understand," I responded.

"Still."

"Don't worry Deacon, its fine. As a matter of fact I have time later today if you wanted to bring Pace." Deacon Brown nodded.

"He is late for school."

"It's already started," I asked him.

"Yeah, he was supposed to start Wedgewood this week. But, I couldn't let him go."

I nodded. I thought that Pace was in a bad situation. He must have looked awful or got a hold of something horrible at summer camp.

"It's nothing to be embarrassed about," I consoled Deacon Brown, "we all get sick."

"Not like this, but I'll bring him by."

After we received our napkins, the rest of the conversation was on various topics from sports, cars, and lawn care. I didn't want to push the issue of Pace anymore. Once we finished I paid for both of us and left. I talked with Rose and told her she could leave early. Deacon Brown was coming later and I planned to talk with him and Pace personally. She was fine with that and tended to her normal duties. After she was finished, she left and I got the office together.

Deacon Brown came with his son Pace. The amazing thing about Pace is that he didn't look sick. He had no scars, lesions, whelps, or bumps. Nothing about Pace seemed like he was sick. There where some scratch marks on his arms and he seemed drained of energy but he had the look of a normal young teenage boy.

"Pace, you remember Pastor Tyrone," Deacon Brown said.

Pace was considerably shorter then his dad. He was also pudgy and had a round face. The young man nodded. He didn't say anything just had this sheepish blank stare.

"How are you doing Pace," I asked. "Everything going okay."

"Am I in trouble," Pace asked.

"No," I responded. "Please sit, the both you." Pace sat down but Deacon Brown paused. He excused himself and said he would be right back from the restroom. Once Deacon Brown left, I made my way to the mini-fridge and cups. "Want any water," I asked Pace. My back was turned to him while pouring water for the both us.

"Why am I here," a voice asked. I would say it was Pace but it sounded so different then the voice from before.

"Your dad is concerned because he said you got sick at summer camp."

"I am not sick," Pace responded. "There is no need for you preacher man."

I thought that statement was unusual and turned around with both cups of water in my hand. I saw Pace with his head tilted back, mouth open, and his eyes looked as though they where rolled in the back of his head.

"Pace, are you okay," I asked.

"I have already told you, we are fine."

The statement alone was scary but how it came out was even more unnerving. Pace's mouth didn't move but the voice came out nevertheless. The room grew grey and felt cold. It was as though another being had entered into the room but it wasn't Deacon Brown.

"Pace," I called out. My mind was rushing. I had never seen anything like this before. I don't even watch movies with paranormal activities.

"Obsidian," it responded.

Before I could hear anything else, I called on the name of Jesus. With studying, I knew that things of this nature come with fasting and praying. I had prayed before meeting with Pace but not fasted. There was no way I knew that Pace's sickness was under the influence of an alternate being. Deacon Brown didn't warn me.

While calling on the name of the Lord, I could hear the being, Obsidian, getting louder and louder. It was as though it was fighting Jesus and wanted to stay within the young man. I had my eyes closed tight. Fist clinched. All I kept doing was calling on the name of Jesus. There wasn't time for flowery prayers or specific verses. All I could do was say the name of Jesus repeatedly.

Finally, there was a rush of wind and then silence. I stopped and opened one eye at a time. Pace was slumped in the chair. I tapped him. Deacon Brown walked in at the same time with his eyes wide open.

"I heard you down the hall," Deacon Brown said. "Are you okay?"

I nodded and slowly tapped Pace. He jerked which startled me but looked around with his normal look. His eyes looked brighter and that cold feeling left. Pace looked at me then around at his dad. He immediately got up and hugged his father.

"I'm back," Pace said in his normal voice.

I sat down and drank one of the glasses of water. There was a constant prayer of thanks going in my mind for God taking care of the situation. God knew that I wasn't prepared but was with me anyhow. Before talking with the two guys, I drank the second glass of water. Both men sat down and thanked me. They where so overjoyed with the release of his son from that spirit. I told them that was God's work. I had very little to do with it.

I know we talk about spirits as far as alcohol but this was different. As I said before, there are a host of issues and problems but I had to know how that young man got a hold of something like that. It has to be very deliberate to get a specific spirit inside you.

"How did it happen," I asked Pace. "How did, you and Obsidian, become one."

Pace looked at his dad then at me. He began how in the springtime, one of his friends heard about the ability to experience music in a completely new way. It dealt with seeing the music and having an experience with the message all at the same time. Obsidian gives people a clearer view of the world and allows them to see and experience music. Pace wanted to have this experience.

One of Pace's friends did some research and found the spirit called Obsidian and his ability to help them grow as people and musicians. Of course, Pace was uncomfortable with this but thought it couldn't be as bad as he thought. The opportunity to bond with Obsidian was the cause of him not going to church as much or participating.

It was at summer camp where they decided to invite Obsidian so they can grow as people. Eight guys got the same cabin and were thrilled to tap into this other realm. Because it was music, they each brought tracks and small players to play them. Most of the songs came from heavy metal and gangster rap. To the group, this would help with unity and everyone to have a similar experience.

Pace went into detail about how they had a special tea blended from Brahami, Jata Mansi herb, Ginko-Bilboa, and Basil. Each person drank the strange brew and drew a part of the pentagram on the main floor. They made sure to be very quiet so their cabin counselor wouldn't come in to break up the meeting. Because they didn't want to disturb him, they didn't use candles, but their cell phones in strategic places around the pentagram.

They played the necessary music softly and begin with the chant that Pace's friend found on the web. Pace felt uncomfortable but continued through the service, until their phones started flickering. Until that point Pace honestly believed there was no way this could work.

Then the lights went out and darkness covered the room. Before they could say anything, a grayish light came from the side of the room and howled through the area. Things shook and beds levitated. The cabin counselor walked in and then ran out when he saw the craziness that was going on.

Pace tried to leave but saw this image rush at him. After the encounter, his vision was as if it was looking through a foggy glass. After that he couldn't escape the mindset of being and the music that they where playing kept replaying in his head. Sometimes to get rid of the thing, he would scratch himself to relieve the mental stress. It wasn't until the Pastor Study that he felt like himself.

Deacon Brown and Pace left after I heard the story. It was shocking and gave me the chills. I actually slept that night with the lights on. I prayed that God would remove what Obsidian said to me in the study. Hearing his voice was something of another realm. The encounter gave me a completely new perspective on evil and even changed my sermons. After that, I implored people to stay away from evil things. Don't go down that alley. Because if it shows up, then be prepared for the unexpected.

It is best to stay away from going onto Satan's Territory.

The Golden Image

112

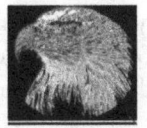

VERSUS

I Samuel 17

"Carlisle, what'cha thinking about?"

I look over at my classmate, Amanda, and smile. "Wedgewood," I respond. The water spray cools our faces as we sit near the falls at Sheridan Falls. This tall natural land structure is what gives the town its name. That and the person who started this city, Brent Sheridan. The falls itself is a tourist attraction, inviting many people from at least 200 miles away to come and see them. Many people come for the falls, and then go to the beach, which is on the other side of town but not that far away.

There are various vendors, bed and breakfasts, and even a museum site on the history of the falls. I've been there many times. When you live here, it's no big deal. Its nothing like Niagara, but it is large at seventy-seven feet tall. Plus, it's one of the few falls in the area. This one is the easiest to get too and not to far from Amanda's and I home.

"Why are you thinking of high school," Amanda responds.

"I'm excited. Looking forward to new things."

A nice breeze comes by. It is refreshing and I can tell by Amanda's grin that she likes it as well. I stare at some tourists going into the small museum by the falls. Inside there are books, pamphlets, cups, souvenirs, and various other items to buy. They make a decent some of money.

"Same here but I'm not trying to rush it," she says.

"I'm glad we're going to the same place."

"We live close to one another," Amanda says and runs her finger through her hair. She cut her hair last week. Throughout my entire time of knowing Amanda, her hair hung down the length of her back. Then for some reason she changed it. Not sure why but she's still cute.

"You know how they do districts around here. It's not as simple as based on your neighborhood or where you live. Tommy, whose a few streets behind us is going to the other school."

"Brent?"

"Yeah, Brent."

Amanda laughs and touches my shoulder. "You're so funny. Already trying to start a rivalry with that school."

"I know its silly, but once you're in one school, you have to start disliking the other. They're our biggest rival in the area."

"True," she says. Her eyes fixate on the ice cream stand that is near us.

"Forget the Unicorns, Ocelots for life." Amanda laughs harder and stares at the ice cream. "You want one?"

"One what?"

She loves playing coy. "Ice cream. I see you staring."

"Don't worry about it."

"C'mon, let's go," I respond. I stand up and hold my hand for her to grab. She plays as if it doesn't matter but then gets up and follows me.

I don't have much money but my parents give me an allowance and I do odd jobs for neighbors. Stuff like cut the grass, yard work, cleaning cars, and other things. It's cool and allows me to have money for occasions like this.

We get our ice cream. The stand has basic flavors. This isn't a problem because both of us like chocolate. We head back to our original seat and see that a few visitors are sitting there. Amanda finds another table for us to relax and enjoy the ice cream. We talk for five minutes when Randal pulls up on his bike. He's alone, which is good and unusual.

Randal is a known pest and bully at our middle school. He usually hangs out with two other guys and they love to mess with various people in class. I can't stand it and am not afraid. Taking up years of marital arts gives me plenty of confidence. Randal, like me, always had his eyes set on Amanda since seventh grade. She can't stand Randal and that's infuriating to him. Excellent. We are not friends, Randal and I, so he has no business stopping by our table.

"Hey lovebirds," Randal says in an annoying voice and makes kissing noises to go along. We ignore him. Maybe he'll just go away. "You don't hear me talking to you, I said hey love…"

"We heard you," I respond.

"Why didn't you…"

"Because it was pointless," I say. "Not worth the time." Amanda nudges her elbow in my side and shakes her head. She knows about Randal's bullying ways and thinks I'm crazy for standing up to him.

Unlike Randal and even Amanda, I have not hit my growth spurt. I know its coming. I'm a little more tired then usual, and my older brothers say that's when they got taller. Being the youngest sibling, I've learned from them. Having two older brothers prepares me a lot about what to expect and how to handle myself against bigger people. I'm sure Amanda is afraid for my safety. I've seen Randal fight. She should be worried for him.

"You being funny, shrimp," Randal says in his most intimidating voice possible. He's actually only about four inches taller. This is a big difference but not a problem.

"No, those are for comedians and clowns. Like yourself."

"Carlisle," Amanda whispers. I know that tone. She doesn't want me to start something publicly.

"It's okay."

"You think, I won't do something don't you," Randal says and steps to my side with both fists clinch. He's close. Too close. I can smell the tuna melt he had earlier in the day.

"I'm sure you will. You're dumb enough to get yourself in trouble," I respond and lick some of my ice cream. That was actually funny.

"Listen here twerp," Randal begins and jabs his finger into my shoulder. That's a mistake and is made worst because he uses his closes arm to me. He starts to say something through grimace teeth. I don't pay any attention and hand Amanda my ice cream.

Before Randal has time to respond to my small gesture I grab the part of his hand between the index finger and thumb. I remember that from Aikido the little spot on the hand is a serious pressure point. A person can bring almost anyone down if you squeeze it hard enough. Randal clinches in pain and I immediately grab his elbow with my other hand to force his body towards the table.

He bangs his head with a thud but is okay. I doubt he'll even have a concussion. I apply pressure to Randal's hand and elbow to hold him in check. He wants to be free but can't. It hurts too much.

"Its okay folks, we're just practicing. Wrestling stuff. Its okay," I yell to people whose looking at us. I'm sure they're wondering what is going on. "Isn't that right," I ask Randal and squeeze the pressure point.

"Yes," Randal grimaces.

Some people take our word for it and stop looking. Amanda even stops licking her ice cream. I smile, wink at her, and return my attention to Randal.

"Listen here, Randal," I say in a control voice. "I'm tired of you thinking you can ruin my life and bullying people. Enough is enough. Understand?"

There was a pause and I apply some pressure. "Yes," Randal responds.

"Good. Now I don't want to hear about you coming after Amanda, or anyone else. Understand?"

"Yes," he says this time much quicker.

"Good. If I let you go, are you going to get on your bike and get out of here, or am I going to have to snap your arm like a chip."

"Carlisle," Amanda says.

I mouth to her that it will be okay and return my attention to Randal. A little pressure on the hand and he responds.

"Yes," he says. "I'll leave."

Satisfy with his answer I let him go. Randal rubs his hand then his elbow. He looks at Amanda and then at me. I wave to the bike and he flinches. He wants to do something stupid. Please Lord; don't let him do something stupid. I'm not in the mood to get in trouble. There was a brief stare down and Randal leaves on his bike.

"Sorry," I say to Amanda. Her mouth is still slightly open. She's in shock at what happened. I take my ice cream from her and lick. "Tasty."

"That was amazing."

"Not really," I say, "I can't stand bullies."

Weeks later, I'm thrilled for high school. Carver and Carlton, my two older brothers, think I'm crazy. They have been there for a few years each. Both are stars in sports so everyone loves them. I would imagine due to their size no one messes with them. They're athletic but so am I. You have to be to earn black belts in Aikido. However, I prefer books and art. There's something about using your mind to handle the situation. Then again, sometimes you have to do a little of both, like in the case of Randal.

Both of them try to scare me. Carver and Carlton says that people will mess with me; I have to be careful for cliques, and try not to embarrass them while in school. They call it giving helpful advice. I enter Wedgewood with a few friends already. One of my friends was Mike, and of course Amanda.

After the incident at the falls, Randal's family moved. I don't think it was because of me. His family planned on moving so I bet that incident at the falls was going to be his last hurrah. That's probably why he paused. He knew if he could hurt me, then it would be okay since he's moving. I'm glad he did the smart thing and rode away on his bike.

The first day was fun. Getting to meet the teachers and finding my middle school friends. Mike's and I lockers are on opposite side of the school. However, Amanda and I had lockers that are only three spots away. It's great knowing someone on the first day being so close. It brings a sort of peace to the mind. The entire day was great, except for the last part. During lunch, I heard about a guy and his friends who bullies or threatens freshmen. Mike said he saw someone turned literally upside down for money. They think it is cool to harass people and I'm not having it.

Amanda keeps me calm after I hear Mike's news. I agree with her that it's none of my business. Besides, I can't go around fighting people at random. Today is my first day at school. No reason to be stupid.

"Learn anything," Amanda says as we pack our book bags getting ready to go home.

"Naw, not really," I respond. "Outside of some basic stuff like, hi I'm Mr. Gary and I'm teaching History."

We both laugh and then turn our attention to a much older student poking some short kid in the face. They are many lockers down from us so I can't hear what they where saying. I know it's not good and the kid is probably being bullied. At least I think.

My first reaction was to walk over to the situation but Amanda grabs my arm. I look at her and nod. Sometimes I need to let it go or else I can be like them. Having the ability to defend the weak can be used to become a bully if that power is not checked. The older teen let the boy go. He got whatever he wanted from the poor kid. Something has to stop this mess. It can't keep going.

Mike walks up to us from behind. For a moment he startles Amanda and I. He nods in the direction of the young guy who walks away after the taller kid left the area.

"Volos," Mike says.

"Who's that," I ask.

"The taller kid, he's one of Volos friends'," Mike says with air quotations around friends. He really meant more like a gang or group of thugs.

"Who names their kid, Volos," Amanda asks.

She said what I was thinking. "Maybe someone who knew he would grow up crazy," I say. We laugh at that and head for the exit. We talk a little more about Volos and his group of friends. I can't believe my brothers never talked about him.

That night I ask my brothers about Volos. They are a little dismissive but say that Volos is a bully who messes with people. Because both of them where on the football and basketball teams, Volos didn't bother them. Volos and his group always seem to target who they believed were weak. Neither one of my brothers thought he was dangerous. They didn't think he was part of a real gang.

I still desire to know more but they did not feel like talking about it. I can't believe they didn't do anything to put an end to his bullying. They did say that Volos was big, but both of my brothers are tall guys. One was a Shooting Guard and the other a tall Wide Receiver. I guess they weren't the biggest guys on the team but I'm still surprised they didn't stop the bullying.

All that week I was asking people about Volos and who he was. I got a variety of information about him. He seems to love fear and get a rush from pushing people around. Some of the teachers knew about the situation but didn't want to do anything about it. I guess two years ago, after a retiring teacher stood up to Volos, he mysteriously found his car scratched with a knife, the tires busted, and raw eggs thrown on the hood.

Many people believe Volos is part of a real gang. Like a true group of gangsters who have guns and sell drugs. For some reason I didn't buy it. Granted it could be true but logic says he should have target a diverse group of people. Especially those with money or could get him better business.

My science teacher is concern for me because of my questions. She does not think it's a good idea for me to ask about Volos. She doesn't want me to get hurt and I listen intently to her advice out of respect. Her words do not sway me from finding Volos and stopping him from bullying the students at Wedgewood High.

At the first football game of the year Carver, the oldest of us three brothers introduce me to some of his friends and the cheerleaders. He starts for the team and is thinking of a few universities to play football. He brings me along to some of the cheerleaders before the game to win points with them. My height makes me look much younger then my age. In reality, I'm not short at all. Both of my brothers are 6'3". I figure eventually that I have to grow, but am proud of my height. One cheerleader in particular was pretty nice, and pretty.

"What's your name," she asks.

"Carlisle," I respond. "Yours?"

"I like that," she says, clearly not responding to my question. "I like that your parents gave 'Car' in all your names," she says to my brother. At least she was observant and correct. Carver was the oldest and named after dad. Carlton is in the middle and a year younger then Carver. I am two years younger then him.

"You know how we do," Carver responds in a voice that is a little deeper then what I'm use to hearing from him.

"I'm Tatiana," she says responding to my question.

"Nice to meet you," I say and hold out my hand.

She looks at my hand for a moment and then shakes it. "You're so proper," Tatiana says in away as if I'm a kid in elementary school. I take it as a complement and leave the area. Carver only wants me there for a brief moment to draw attention and then go away. It's cool. I have friends to meet up with anyway.

I meet Mike and Amanda in the stands and we wait for our football team, the Ocelots, to come out to the field. There is a guy in an Ocelot costume near the cheerleaders pumping up the crowd. I hear they use to have a real one, until it was freaked out by the band and jumped on its handler. I'm sure it wasn't a pretty sight but it would have been great to see a real Ocelot. I'm sure Carver made his way to the team as well as Tatiana to her squad. Everyone is wearing purple or grey as we cheer our team. We play against some poor sap of a school that's being dominated.

After the first quarter, Amanda had a taste for some popcorn and possibly ice cream. Not sure what's up with her and this ice cream but that's what she wants. We tell Mike that we'll be right back and head for the concessions. On the way, we walk behind the stands and on a worn path. Some tall muscular teen was heading for us with four guys around him.

I nod in their direction and lead Amanda away from them and towards the concession. I didn't want to walk further underneath the bleachers and run into the guys. Then it dawns on me, one of them looks familiar.

"Hey kid," the one in the middle says.

I stop and look. I hold Amanda tightly, making sure she will be okay. I see the guy who calls out to me but look past his shoulder to a familiar face. He is the same guy from earlier in the week that harassed the freshman at the locker.

"Heard you looking for me," he says. This must be Volos. He is tall and quite muscular. He seems like he should be a power forward for a college team. The guys around him were not as big but they had some decent size.

"Maybe," I respond. "What's your name," I ask. I know already but it's cool to be polite.

"Volos," he responds with almost a shot of arrogance. "Yours."

"Carlisle," I say. "This is Amanda, nice to meet you." With that, we begin to make our way around the group until one of his guys gets closer to cut us off. Instinctively I stop Amanda and back up. This time we're getting a little closer to the bleacher. It has a variety of steel beams crisscrossed for strength. I have an idea, but doubt it would work.

"Where you going kid," Volos friend says as he walks to us. "The little missy looks nice," he laughs.

"We don't want any trouble just ice cream and popcorn," I warn. He doesn't pay any attention to that and keeps coming. His friends chuckle some and the closet guy has his eyes on Amanda. I doubt they'll do anything stupid but he wants to scare me. Not happening.

Amanda and I stop and the guy keeps coming until I know he's with in striking distance. Without warning to Amanda, I release her and kick the man just below his knee. I meant to get his ankle but missed. The results played out a little better then expected.

The guy immediately fell and went face first into the side of the bleachers. I thought he might stumble which would allow me to strike again. However, that was unnecessary since he fell into the bleacher. The steel rings and the man fall back with blood spewing from his mouth.

I have to admit, that makes me nervous. He is in clear pain and shakes from the hit. I look at Volos who was in shock and then Amanda. "Let's go," I say and we both take off to the concession stand. I can tell Volos was irate and wants to do something but has to take care of his friend.

After the incident, we head back to Mike and told him we had something to say. We didn't want to say anything then, because I knew people in the crowd would hear. Volos probably got his friend some help. I cannot imagine him telling anyone out of shear embarrassment. I do know there will be some retaliation. It's okay. I'm still not scared.

The following Monday at study hall I sit next to someone new. At Wedgewood, study hall can be in various places around building. In this case, it's in the balcony of the auditorium, which is strange. It's quiet, and with no assembly not a bad place for a large group of people. Still, inside the auditorium gives a different feel. Amanda and I both share the same study hall and sit near the new person.

"My name is Carlisle, yours," I ask the guy. He's a little pudgy and seems to have an aura of quietness. The new guy is shy, like there's a reason. It is as if fear is driving him to silence.

"Pace," he responds.

"I'm Amanda." He smiles at both of us.

"This is my first day," Pace says. "Wedgewood is big."

"Yeah," I say. "I like the new improvements that they made. At least it's now up to par with Brent."

"That's nice," Pace responds.

We all keep our voices down so we don't distract others and the teacher at the other end of the room. We talk about a variety of things from sports, schools, and even music. The last topic is strange because Pace is strict on the types of music he listens too. It's only Gospel and Christian for now. He doesn't go into the reason, but describes that he had a bad experience with secular music. Pace knows that he doesn't want to go down that road again. We all have our standards and I can't blame him.

During the conversation, a familiar form walks over. He looks larger in clear light. I can tell Volos isn't pleased but he's not going to start trouble. Too many people. He's not a stupid bully, just a mean one.

Volos sits right next to Amanda and me. He's near Pace but doesn't pay any attention to him.

"You lucky," Volos begins.

"No, my name is Carlisle, but I have trouble with names as well," I respond. Amanda bows her head knowing I'm urging the guy on.

"Don't play games with me," Volos responds. He's grimacing through his teeth and spit is forming in the corners of his mouth. "You could've seriously hurt Martin."

I stare at Amanda and then at Pace. They don't know Martin so I look at Volos then shrug my shoulders. Volos looks around and sighs hard.

"The guy whose head you slammed into the bleachers."

"Actually he fell, which I didn't mean to cause," I respond.

"You know what I mean," Volos yells. The room grows quiet and not a word is spoken. The teacher in study hall looks at us and begins to walk over.

"Oh I thought you meant the Titans in Tennessee, I didn't realize you meant the ones in Homer's epic," I say aloud. The teacher stops and puts his finger to his lips. He wants us to be quiet and I nod. Volos is confused and doesn't know what happened. "The teacher was coming, you're welcome."

"Don't be alone," Volos says while pointing his thick finger in my face. "We're watching you. Don't think your brothers can protect you from me," he says. "Not even God, can protect you from me."

Before I respond, Volos gets up and walks out of study hall. Pace stares at me for a brief moment with shock in his face. "What was that about," he asks.

"Nothing much," I respond. "He's mad 'cause I gave his friend some serious dental reconstruction." Pace pauses. "Don't worry, I'm not violent. Really, I'm not, but he's a bully. And I can't stand bullies."

"I feel you," Pace responds. He looks down at his books lost in thought. I'm not sure what he's thinking about but I know it wasn't great.

Amanda is scared for my safety the rest of the day. She assumes that at any given moment Volos and crew will attack. They didn't. I can't get over what he said. 'Not even God can save me'. That's courage. I can't believe he would have the gall to say that. Actually when he said it, my heart flipped. I thought a lighting bolt would strike him down in study hall.

A week goes by and no retaliation from Volos or his friends. That's cool and maybe Volos has calmed down. Besides, I actually didn't want to get into a fight. That could lead to a suspension. That's not how I plan to start a promising high school career. My parents would be mad and not happy that I took my Aikido and Muy Tai Boxing training to hurt people. They only allowed me to do that because they wanted me to be active, like Carver and Carlton.

During the third week of school, I hang out near the falls with my guitar. I'm not looking for money but it's peaceful. For some reason I like it more then the beach. Granted both are tourist attractions but my favorite is the falls. They are soothing and relaxing. Also, I like that a bridge was created to take visitors ten feet away from the falling water. I'm away from the bridge and sitting to the side enjoying some tunes that I learned from youtube. It's great that I can learn popular songs from that site.

Riding up on her bike is Amanda. I'm surprise to see her and wave. She smiles and rolls up to my side. "Hey Amanda," I say.

"Hi," she responds. We talk for a bit but I can tell that something is on her mind. Instead of drawing the conversation out, I ask and she responds. "I'm concerned for you."

"Volos?"

"Yeah," she says. "I know you have martial arts skills but I don't want you to rely on that to prove a point."

"I'm not," I respond. "Volos is our Goliath."

"Goliath?"

"Yeah, remember David and Goliath?"

"Yes," Amanda says. "But what does that have to do with us."

"Goliath was just a big bully. He was trying to push people around and David couldn't stand for that. Especially when he made fun of God. David knew something had to be done. A lesson had to be taught."

"Like Volos," she says.

"Sort of yeah. I mean, he's not evil, but I've heard some things on him. I've been digging and there are many scared kids around here. They have been hurt, beaten, robbed, and messed over. Plus Volos is secretly training a younger crew to continue his madness once he graduates."

"That's crazy," Amanda whispers.

"Exactly. I don't want to fight. I'll even try reasoning with him, but in case that doesn't work, then..." I say and pause. She knows what I mean. I strum a few notes on the guitar and Amanda sings along. Like clockwork, someone hands her a bill. We thank the person and sing a few more songs. After we collect enough money, we get ice cream and sodas.

The next day the art teacher, Mr. Walznick, allows me to go and straighten the room. There's a brief break in the middle of day where the art class isn't being used. Sometimes I go there instead of study hall. I tell Amanda and Pace where I am so they don't worry that Volos came and killed me. Can't have her scared for my well-being all the time.

While straightening the art room I hear the door open from behind. I didn't think anything of it, figuring its Mr. Walznick. "Thanks for the opportunity to straighten up. I'm learning about the variety of art materials in the room."

"What opportunity," the voice says. I pause while putting the paints back in their proper place. I recognize the voice.

"Hey Volos," I respond and turn around. He wasn't alone. Martin, whose face healed nicely but has a definite scar, and three other guys are with Volos. "Martin," I say to the scar face guy. "Sorry about," I point to my face and then his.

"You're gonna' suffer," Martin responds. Apology not accepted.

"I have to warn you by law that I've trained in Aikido martial arts for self defense." The group pauses. I can tell by their movements that they clearly don't care. They are trying to circle me but that's not happening.

Immediately I go to my right and towards Martin. This forces him to swing at me which I dodge and grab his other wrist. By applying pressure, I immediately twist his arm and flip him into a table. With unbelievable luck, Martin's face slams into the table and is out cold.

Another guy comes at me I flip him across the table. I see a third guy on the other side of a different table and kick that so it hits him in the stomach. That buys me time to jump on the nearest table and run at the guy who attacked second.

He sees me coming and swings wildly. I have the high ground and jump over his useless punch. After landing, I kick him in the back of the leg and grab his wrist. "Also I learned a little Muy Tai Boxing for attacks, which uses a lot of elbows and knees," I grimace while using my elbows and knees on the last three syllables of my warning.

Two down and three to go. Volos is standing by the door in shock. Two of his friends are out cold and the other two will join them soon.

The guy closest to Martin runs at me with scissors and a paint brush. I take a chair and toss it at his feet. His friend joins him from the side and the guy with the weapons tries to jump over it. He trips and falls on the scissors. Thankfully, it punctures his shoulder. He screams and I quickly kick him in the head to silence him.

The last of Volos friend thought to use the distraction as an opportunity. They still have not learned that Aikido is all about using your opponent's aggression against them. These guys are almost making it to easy. I immediately flip the guy on the table and come down hard with my elbow across his face.

Footsteps come from behind and of course, Volos, the coward, makes his move now. I know how tall he is and drive my elbow towards my back. I hit him in the stomach and swing around to punch him in the side and then knee him in the back.

Volos was tough. Most guys would have gone down immediately but he stood there in obvious pain. I wonder if I caught him in the kidneys. I hope not. Volos looks at the scissors and picks them up. He swings a few times which is dangerous. He has a huge wingspan and can move very fast.

Finally, Volos makes an error and swings the scissors down. He gets it caught in the table. I immediately kick him in the side of the knee and grab his free arm. With all my strength, I hold his elbow and push up on his wrist. Volos face slams into the table. He's in pain but not unconscious.

"This is crazy," I say. He's struggling to free himself but I apply more pressure. Too much more and his arm will break. "Volos, Volos," I call. He stops for a moment and breathes. "Look at you. Look at your broken friends. Is this who you are? Is this what you want in life," I ask. He's silent and in clear pain. "You're better then this. You know that. Wake up from being this stupid. Wake up."

I let him go. His hand is close to the scissors. Volos could reach for it and stab me in the chest. He doesn't. I hear what sounds like small whimpers. Volos is remembering who he is and trying not to cry. I walk away. Now is his time for reflecting, not for me to gloat. Before leaving, I inform Volos that there's a class next period. They might want to be gone by then.

Volos must have left for the rest of the day. Amazingly some people heard a little of what happened in the art room and news spread about me defeating his crew. I didn't confirm or deny anything but the school knew. Amanda was proud of me for not trying to publicize the event and figure that I didn't lead them into the room to attack.

We did not see Volos or his crew for a few days. Now I'm a little concerned. I hope that no one was severely injured. Often I replay the fight in my mind making sure that I didn't permanently hurt anyone. Except for Martin, I'm not sure how that scar is going to heal across his face. I believe everyone should be okay.

The day before the big football game, I'm with Amanda and Pace in study hall. I didn't clean the art class everyday but twice week. Mr. Walznick never knew what happened exactly but said the day of the fight that the class looked fantastic. That makes me feel good. At least it meant that Volos and friends cleaned up what they could. That is after they woke up.

Amanda, Pace, and I are talking about plant biology when the room went silent. I look at the door and see Volos heading our way. He didn't have a sneer or angry look but sadness. Please don't let one of the guys be paralyzed or worst, dead. Volos sits in the row in front of us.

"I woke up," Volos says. Amanda and Pace does not know what that means but I do. I stick out my hand to shake but he gave me a hug. "Thank you." I was speechless, didn't know what to say. We sat back down and sighed. "When it was us versus you, I learned a lot."

"Same here," I respond. "But I'm here for you. We all are," I say inviting Amanda and Pace's friendship with Volos. They nod but are clearly confused.

"Good to know," Volos responds.

He informs me that the other guys where fine. Martin will heal which is a blessing but transferred to some private school. He's tired of being embarrassed. I understand that. The other guys are okay but do have random headaches. I must have hit them hard in the head and apologize for that and will say so in person the next time they're at school.

One of the guy's parents thought about pressing charges but because they came in as a group, I could easily claim self-defense. One of them even tried to use a weapon, which could land him in jail. I agree not to press charges and let that moment pass, but I did have one condition. No more bullying. Volos agrees.

Right before study hall was over Volos open up about himself. We didn't learn a lot about his life, but from his words, I can tell he's abused at home. I'm not sure if it's more neglect or mental. He needs confidence and real friends. I agree to be there for him and help if possible. Also before leaving, I encourage him that he can be great, so he wouldn't feel the need to hurt others and bring them down to his level.

As we walk out of study hall, people around us are amazed. My mind left them and is curious about Pace and his strong abhorrence of various music. I ask him about it and he responds.

"Trust me," Pace says, "you don't want to know that story."

"Try me," I say.

Stand up to bullies because in doing so you might help others.

THE GOLDEN IMAGE

Daniel 3

Part I

The morning forest came alive with the fresh scent of dew and soil in the air. There's dampness in the air. It covers the clothes and filters into your lungs. The air presses my body but makes me sharp, especially for the sport at hand.

Paintball is fun, but not my favorite activity. I remember the first time I played. Everyone told me that its fun and it wouldn't hurt. It was fun, but they lied about the not hurting part. Granted the vest protects the internal organs, but my extremities took a beating. This time I'm prepared. I made sure to wear extra clothes under my pants and shirt, even though it's the start of July. The cooling air is refreshing for this time of year.

As a group, we need this fun time activity. We have been working all year long on Vice President Jason Templeton's presidential candidacy. To most on the staff, he's a shoe-in to win because of his overwhelming popularity while being the vice president. Still V.P. Templeton does not take this lightly and wants to show America that he's serious about running the country.

Vice President Templeton told us, his staff, a story about an event that formed his life. Twenty-five years ago, he chose the wrong prom date and it almost landed him in prison. From there he learned to put himself in the best position to flourish. He's very thankful that his friend at the time, now current wife, was there for him through the accusation.

A hand touches my arm and then covers my mouth to muffle the scream. I turn around to see Aaron Trudeau Jr. We call him AJ because he's named after his dad. AJ is very proud to carry his father's name. Aaron senior survived an avalanche with a few other people from my hometown of Sheridan Falls on Mount Cadeyrn. AJ figured the survival gene is strong in his family, which will help in this game of paintball.

"You gotta be more aware Sherwood," AJ says. I nod. AJ thinks he's some military specialist because he watches war movies and plays video games. "Those Zebras could've gotten you."

Our staff decides to split in two different teams with Vice President Templeton joining in the fun. He's in his 40's and great physical shape. Because of his high ranking, our paintball team colors are gold and white instead of neon green and blue. The gold and white is homage to the Brent High Unicorns, which like him, was my alma mater as well.

The Zebras, or Ice Zebras, shoot the white balls where our team has the gold. We named ourselves the Golden Stags. Kind of strange, but it makes it more fun.

"Your uncle is no joke and will pop you on site," AJ whispers. By Uncle, he means Vice President Templeton. At family functions, I call him Uncle Jason, but at work, it's all business. Most of the staff doesn't know my relationship with him because I don't want to be treated differently.

Aunt Marcy, Uncle Jason's wife, is the younger sister to my dad, Felix. Uncle Jason and I are close but his job kept him away from Sheridan Falls most of the time. I did get to hang out with my cousin, Jarius, who is the V.P.'s only son. Even though Jarius didn't go to Brent, we are still close and he joined his father's staff as well. The paintball outing was his idea.

"I know," I tell AJ. "Trust me, I'm vigilant. Glad Jarius is on our team."

AJ smiles and nods. He starts to stand and points to himself and then towards the left. He points to me and then to the right. I understand what he wants. AJ and I go in our separate ways with our paintball guns ready. We're looking for anyone in the general military fatigues given by the company and vests with the white matching arm bands. We all have helmets with eye shields. Vice-President Templeton can't have people going blind during a fun excursion while he runs for the highest office.

I see something white in the distance and shoot a few rounds. Then my heart skips, someone took their extra white band and tied it to the tree. Once I realize my mistake, I immediately drop and roll but am hit three times in the leg.

Even with the extra pants that still stung. I roll some more and look in the direction of where the shots were fired. Jessica Rodriguez is running at me with her gun aimed and ready. I reach for my weapon and she fires more paintballs. It hits my gun, arm, shoulder, and a few in the chest.

"I'm done," I yell. She has me. I stop reaching for the gun. I can't see her deep brown eyes through the visor, but know she is very happy.

Jessica comes from a military background. Her grandfather and dad were in the army. She herself joined the Navy to take after her mom's profession. Jessica is older then me by seven years but hangs out with most of the staff closer to my age.

I look to my right and past her shoulder. She can't see my eyes focus on an image behind her because of the shields. I see a teammate of mine and they are waiting. On my back, I lift my hands up.

"A little help," I ask.

"Sure," Jessica responds. She points her gun up with one hand and helps me stand with the other. I slowly get up realizing how much my leg hurts. Being shot like that isn't fun.

"Thanks Jessica, you're real good at..." before I can finish Jessica looks at my visor and sees someone running in our direction.

Jessica turns around and fires but misses her target. The person running, my teammate does not. She's shot three times in the chest and knows it's over.

"Thanks Sherwood," Jarius says.

"Anytime."

"Is that anyway to treat your girlfriend," Jessica says.

Jarius walks in close, grabs Jessica from the back, and pulls her close. He gently presses his helmet against hers symbolizing a kiss.

"You can take the helmets off for a brief moment, idiot," Jessica says playfully. Jarius laughs some and takes her up on the suggestion. They kiss and put their helmets on.

"Meet you back at H.Q.," Jarius says. He crouches some and run back in the same direction he came from. Jessica and I look at one another and sigh. We walk back in the direction of the Safety zone, or H.Q. as Jarius calls it, with our hands in the air. This is the place where we can go and wait for the other 'killed' players.

"That was a nice play you did," Jessica says.

"You shot me."

"But asking for help to get up, smart."

"My leg does hurt," I respond. "Look at me, I'm limping."

Jessica waves her hand in disgust. "Please that's nothing. You should see some of the scars on my leg from service."

I pause and then sigh. "I bet its something," I say.

"Especially on my calf."

"Cool."

"You think Vice President Templeton will win," Jessica asks. "I like my job and talking with Jarius, he seems real passionate about helping America."

"He's great," I respond. "I know its July, but his popularity is huge. He can almost do anything and the people will back him."

"You're right. That makes more sense."

"What does," I ask. We continue walking through the forest zone getting closer to the safety area.

"Hmm, not sure if I should say," Jessica begins, "but you're close to Jarius and V.P. Templeton."

"Yeah, you can say that," I respond. She doesn't know that I'm family. Jarius was going to tell everyone but I asked him not too. Only AJ knows and that's because he knew me before the political office.

"Vice President Templeton is working on a new vision of America."

"Every president, or should I say, all new presidents has their ideas."

"No, this is big. Country altering," Jessica responds.

"Like how Lincoln changed America," I ask jokingly.

"Yes."

I stop. She pauses with me. She can tell I'm in shock but we both continue. "What are you talking about? Are there slaves?"

"Not like that Sherwood," Jessica says. "But Templeton will unify this country. He's tired of what has happened. Now that current President Randolph got the country in great economic standing, Templeton will lead it to where it's supposed to be. According to him."

"I see," I say with some confusion.

We enter the safety zone and grab some sodas. It has the look of a ski lodge with most of the décor wood and plaid. A large fireplace is at the back of the building with the drinks area to the left. A group of couches, chairs, and tables are near the windows on the side of the building. Beyond the back doors is where our gear will go as well as the debriefing center and safety instructions.

Jessica and I meet up with other co-workers with various paint stains. We're taking our time before changing out our paintball gear. It looks like there are a few more Zebras then Stags so I'm hoping we'll win. After sipping on a red soda, my thoughts go to what Jessica told me. My mind is trying not to worry, but begins to think about what Uncle Jason is planning. I just hope it's only a fairy tale and not real.

My legs are sore but I make my way to a couch near the window. I sip some more on the soda and sigh. I hope Vice President Templeton is not doing what I have heard. I can't imagine my political career starting with his unity plan. In Lincoln's time, the issue was political and civil rights. What possible way will my Uncle unify the country? I sit for a moment sip on the soda while looking out the window. The answer hits my mind faster then Jessica snuck up on me. I think I know his plan for America and I do not like it.

Part 2

As with any country that thrives, change must occur. Most empires that succeed do so because of great adaptation to uncontrolled changes around them. They foster change so their citizens can thrive. It can be because of a pandemic disease so new sanitation forms come around to clean the streets. It is possible through wars that new means of picking a leader comes about to please the citizens. Financial collapse can bring about the means to help people. Even religious institutions can promote change in laws and government.

Nations and empires rise or fall because of internal issues. America has endured a variety of problems. Issues such as natural disasters, diseases, financial collapse, and attacking external forces have harmed the country. In spite of this, the country continued to grow. The one time it almost fell apart was during the civil war in the 1860's.

Currently nothing is that serious, but there is still angst brewing amongst the citizens. People can only be so understanding and welcoming. Eventually kindness is mistaken as weakness and the citizens will eventually revolt. No one wants to be trampled under foot, especially not in their own home.

While I was young, people grew tired of putting their religious beliefs to the side. It was embarrassing for them to have to deny who you are just so others feel comfortable. Over time, this feeling grew more and many people began to lash out.

During my first year of high school, the country was going through another economic turmoil. They were desperate to survive as well as the rest of the world. There was a division amongst the citizens in how the country is governed. An experienced Senator, Woodrow Randolph and his upstart running mate Congressman Jason Templeton provided the key to help the country and unify it. They had tactics aimed at the people on both sides of the political spectrum. Once the people respected the leaders, then Congress had to go along with their plans. This was an amazing feat considering this angered and overjoyed people of both parties.

The Randolph-Templeton ticket was a huge achievement as the economic success of the country grew. The prosperity during the eight years of Jason Templeton's Vice Presidency makes him a popular candidate for the Presidential election. Jason Templeton knew that with great prosperity came a wealth of debauchery.

During the last year and half as Vice President, Jason Templeton became closer to Christian leadership from all backgrounds. Now that the country was financially strong, it was time to be the spiritual beacon for the world. To him, American was supposed to be something greater then just a strong military and financial wealth center. It is suppose to be an example to all other nations on what it means to be under God's authority.

I know on the campaign trail, Vice President Templeton spoke with many ministers, bishops, pastors, and other clergy to get a firm hold on morality. At first, I assumed it was because of his desire to be closer to God. That's understandable to have a moral compass when gaining more power. Often times it's too late once you're in a leadership role.

Something different is going on with Uncle Jason's goal. Jessica confirmed that there is a secret plan but didn't go into further details. I know that after this paintball game the one person I have to talk too. My cousin, Jarius Templeton.

The game ended with out team winning. Apparently, it was down to Jarius and his dad. None of the Golden Stags was willing to shoot the Vice President. Usually they would hesitate allowing the V.P. to almost single-handily destroy our team. Luckily, Jarius, and surprisingly AJ, knocked off most of the Zebras.

Jarius was especially happy that I was able to get Jessica distracted. That maneuver saved the team. I tried explaining to him that it wasn't on purpose but he didn't believe me.

After we celebrate at the safety zone, Jarius and I went to a quiet spot to talk. I didn't want to make it seem serious and draw the attention of our co-workers. On the staff, Jarius is Jason Templeton's marketing and public relations person. I was more of a data collector and paid attention to polls and citizens reactions. Jarius would know more about Uncle Jason's motives. Not only because of his job but he was his son as well.

"I knew you had to be the one," I say to Jarius. "No one else but me would splatter Uncle Jason."

Jarius laughs. "True. That's because we're family. Still keeping that a secret?"

"Yeah," I respond.

"I don't think people will change, but if you insist."

"I do," I say and smile. "Quick question."

"What's up?"

"I see Uncle Jason is hanging around a lot clergy types. That's great," I say to start my thought. "Is it some kind of personal thing or he wants to show the county he's really moral or…" I didn't say anything else. The idea is to let it hang and Jarius to fill in the blank.

Jarius smiles and answers. "It's big cuz'. Real big."

"Involving ministers?"

"Yeap," Jarius says and looks around. He guides me to a corner of the room and begins. "Dad is going to revolutionize this country."

"That's great."

"Extremely."

"How," I ask. Sometimes we talk with big words and great ideas. In reality most of it cannot be done. It's too tough and the opposition is strong. This isn't a dictatorship.

"He is going to unify the country." I pause. He can tell I'm confused and pat me on the back. "I mean really unify the country."

"More so then Lincoln?"

"Lincoln had to unite the country politically. I'm talking spiritually."

"Excuse me."

"We're going to be a nation under God and mean it. No more being ashamed at being a Christian. People are calling for it. They've been calling for it."

"Oh," I respond. It's what I thought. They want to blend church and state and bring God back more prominently. There are many people upset at the removal of the Ten Commandments from judicial buildings and others angry with 'In God We Trust' being removed for money. Prayer is silenced in schools, which got people incensed. I don't think you can force people to with hold their beliefs forever and expect them to take it. I nod and Jarius continues.

"That's right Sherwood. We're bringing God back to this land. It's what people want."

"People want the Lord in their lives and in government," I ask.

"Yes," Jarius responds. "Think about how many people vote based on moral character. We're going through an economic explosion thanks to God."

"True," I respond. Jarius interrupts before I was going to finish my thought.

"And how do we thank Him, by removing God from our schools, workplace, money, and even our minds," Jarius says while tapping his head. "It stops with this administration."

"Wow," I start, "that's pretty intense. You plan on blending the government and church."

"Blend?" Jarius chuckles. "We are going to obliterate that line."

"You think people will go for it?"

"They already have," Jarius answers. Let me tell you a secret to power and control.

"Okay."

"Many films about the future where the government takes over are based on fear. If you scare people then they give up their rights and the government can do as they please."

"True, I like those films," I say.

"Everyone does, but it never last. Fear goes away and common sense returns. So, unless you continue with fear you'll always have uprisings."

"But of course. The people grow weary of too much control."

"Exactly, but, if people want change? If citizens honestly desire to be controlled, then they love you and those in charge. No uprisings. No trouble."

"You'll always have rebels."

Jarius smiles and shakes his head. "Traitors, basically. If people love the law, government, or the leadership, then it won't matter."

"Why," I ask.

"Because the citizens will take care of the rebels for you."

"That sounds deep," I respond. And scary. I still can't understand why the clergy leaders. "One last question."

"Sure, and make sure you don't tell anyone what I told you," Jarius says.

I make the hand motion as though I'm zipping my lips. "Why the ministers? He's talking to all faiths."

"That's simple," Jarius responds. "If we keep Christianity in its current state you'll never have unity," Jarius answers.

"You mean with the different denominations," I say.

"Yeap."

"So..."

"You combine them," Jarius says with no effort.

"Combine them," I ask.

"Yes. Combine them. Make one dominate belief. Combine the best and various parts of all denominations and get the religious leader to hammer it home."

"Oh my goodness."

"I know, genius right," Jarius says. "I thought of it myself and passed it on to dad. He loves the idea."

"What about freedom of religion."

"That's a concept, devised to separate us from God and each other. Trust me, it'll be better for all Americans," Jarius responds.

"One Christian religion."

"That's right. We will all be unified as one nation under God, in divisible, with liberty, and justice for all. It's so beautiful, it almost hurts," Jarius says and laughs as he walks away.

I'm weary about a blend of state and church. They want a state run religion. What's crazy is that if the ministers spread the message to their parishioners of the one belief it could work. In a few years, we will lose our right to choose and I would have helped the man to do it.

Part 3

One year after the paintball game, things went as I expected. Vice President Templeton, my Uncle, won the presidency. The office was happy and thrilled at the outcome. It was the largest presidential election victory in at least a hundred years. People really bought in to his message of a unified America.

Due to the election, there was widespread growth in churches. The ministers who Uncle Templeton spoke with, was doing a great job at influencing their membership. In the past year, Christians of all denominations began to see the similarities of their beliefs instead of the differences. For the first time people began to enjoy different doctrines as long as it was tied to God.

As with any change, there were rebels. Not everyone was thrilled with a strong push for religious change. Many believed it was against the constitution. President Templeton was able to overcome that during his previous term as vice president. President Randolph appointed three sympathetic Supreme Court judges that viewed the constitution similar to him. These three officials where important in being able to get the government connect with religious organization and charities. The union between the government and religious charities, allowed the county to set up central mandates. These laws guided the charities and organizations to follow the new countrywide orders of one supreme unity.

People where ecstatic at President Templeton's victory. I'm a part of the group who helped him be elected. I should feel great but have a feeling as if something bad is brewing. In spite of the wide spread joy across the county, there is a serious growing hostility to this new order. They believe that moving the county to one religious order is not what the Founding Fathers had in mind. To combat that idea, President Templeton said, 'There is one supreme Father who founded the world, and that is who I take my lead from.' Interesting.

AJ feels the same way I do. We decide to meet the day before Independence Day near the Washington Monument. With so many people already in town to celebrate the country's birthday, no one from the office would think anything about us meeting there. We can even scout the area for any potential danger sports since President Templeton will have a speech tomorrow on the steps of the Lincoln Memorial.

Inside our office, there are too many ears. Too many people listen and wonder if someone is a traitor or rebel. That thought came from Jarius. For the most part the staff of the president is unified. We support Uncle Jason; however, Jarius is convinced that someone might turn on his father. I think his paranoia is from watching too many political films.

AJ shows up five minutes after me. Both of us marvel at the giant Washington Monument. After a pause, we walk to the World War 2 Memorial and look at the states and golden stars.

"Each one represent so many men," AJ says to break the silence. "Amazing."

"True," I respond. "You think times where simpler then?"

"What do you mean?"

"A clean well defined enemy. Now it's different."

"I'm sure it was the same then. It was clear to many that the Nazi's where an enemy to the world. However, in America people had varying degrees of freedoms and equality."

"True," I respond.

"Life is never easy. Never simple," AJ says.

"Save now," I respond. AJ stops and looks at me. He's wondering if I'm serious. "I'm joking."

"I was wondering if you were serious. Life is never perfect. I'm just surprised."

"At what," I ask

"That the country is coming together, spiritually."

We head in the direction of the Lincoln Memorial. Neither of us is in a rush so we deicide to take the path going around the reflecting pool. The Korean Memorial is one of my favorites. I convince AJ to walk in that direction.

"I'll admit your Uncle has done a great job with that."

"I'm surprised. You think there's a possibility of a one-religion nation?" It dawns on me that there are several countries based on one religion. "I mean for America to become a one religion nation. Almost like a, theocracy."

"Mmm, I don't know. Maybe his speech will influence that," AJ responds.

"Those are words," I respond. "It's tough to convince people with that alone."

AJ nods in agreement. We get to the Korean Memorial and I stand in awe at the soldiers and the wading pool. Each soldier looks ready and determined to fulfill his mission. I'm about to comment on the memorial when a faint voice comes from the Lincoln Memorial.

"You hear that," AJ asks. It isn't uncommon to hear people speak from the Lincoln Memorial. It's a crowd but this sounds like a bullhorn. Almost like someone is making a speech.

"Was there a speech today or a rally," I ask

"No."

Both of us run from the Korean to the Lincoln Memorial. They're not far from each other but getting through the people was tough. We see the Lincoln Memorial is cleared of people except for five standing by the poles. One guy has a bullhorn and there are a few officer making their way to them. The group wants the area to be clear. For a moment, I couldn't figure out what they're doing until it happened.

The man with the bullhorn yells something about stopping the progress of tyranny. Then a bright light and a wave of air came from the front of the memorial. All five people have high-octane explosives around their bodies. The explosion is huge and leads me to believe that it's not an ordinary explosive. The force from all five bombs is powerful.

They used an unknown mixture to create some kind of a low-grade super-explosive. Like a 'daisy cutter' or MOAB bomb but for people. That should have been obvious when the people all jumped to the ground to trigger the explosion.

Pieces of the memorial are flung in the air and crowd. People close to the blast is thrown back. AJ and I were running and it knocks us off our feet. Dust particles and screams fill the air. It makes sense why they wanted the platform cleared. It wasn't in their minds to kill anyone but themselves. After ten minutes, the air settles and the Lincoln is different then before. It's strange to see the memorial with pieces of the poles missing. It's too dark inside the memorial, but I'm hoping Lincoln himself was not affected. Many officers ran to various parts of the memorial looking for injured people.

"What was that," AJ yells. AJ knows our ears are ringing from the explosion. Didn't notice it until he begin talking to me. He said aloud what many people felt. Confusion and panic spreads through the crowd. A couple of park rangers helps the wounded and calms others. Pieces of bodies, granite, and explosive residues are the only thing around the front of the Memorial. No one around the wreckage is alive. No one in the crowd is dead.

Before an all clear is given, the Officers and Rangers run from the stairs as the front of the building collapse. The remaining pieces of poles cannot hold the weight of the roof above them. The entire memorial didn't fall only a part, but that was still dust inducing and loud. There was a huge amount of dirt and debris in the air and more screams. After the dust settles, it is clear that the worst is over. Now it's time to help people.

AJ makes a call back to the office while I help with the people who are wounded. Most people are in shock but not seriously injured. After we help whom we can, AJ and I make our way back to the office.

On the way, we agree not to talk about why we are truly out there. We came because of our mutual problem with the direction of the country. Both of us assume the attack is in retaliation to President Templeton's speech. We were right that not everyone likes his 'One Nation Under God' speech schedule for tomorrow. Rebels are alive and well.

I do see the benefits of my Uncle's dream to unify the country. My problem is forcing people to do it. I feel God has the power to force us to believe He exists. Even though that's how I feel I still don't agree with blowing up a memorial and injuring hundreds. There are other ways to protest.

Once we are at the office various members of the staff and Jarius greet us. Many people clap much to AJ and I confusion but we accept the applause. We helped some people at the Memorial, but they couldn't have known that. Maybe some of it got on the news. Not sure.

"Glad to see you're well," Jarius says.

"Happy to be alive," I respond.

For a few minutes, there are various questions on how we are doing. Many are surprise that we happened to be there. It was for a lunch break is what we say. This is part right but not the entire truth. Running into rebels was unplanned.

Jarius takes us into a room with the President on speaker from his office. Both wanted to know what we saw on the ground. As soon as we walk into the office, Jarius is on his laptop. Apparently, at the times of their deaths the martyrs had a video set up and ready to go on their website. President Templeton is in Georgia to talk about jobs coming to the Southeast.

"What did you see," Jarius asks.

"Five guys, or people, standing by the poles."

Jarius nods and writes what I have to say. "Okay."

"AJ and I were by the Korean Memorial when we heard something like a bull horn. By the time we go to Lincoln, we see the tourists cleared from the area."

"So no one was inside the memorial," the President asks.

"Not from what we can tell," AJ answers. "I doubt they kept those in the store." Inside the Lincoln Memorial is a small store that sold little items and souvenirs based around Abraham Lincoln. Many other memorials had similar stores or places to buy items based on their people as well. Franklin Delano Roosevelt, Jefferson, and Martin Luther king have these similar types of stores near their memorials.

"They must of did it quickly because the main leader said something about tyranny and the rebellion, then explosion," I say.

"Jarius, you said you had something," President Templeton says.

"Yes sir."

Jarius plays from his laptop the rebels video from their website. On it was their reason for the attack on the Lincoln Memorial. They wanted to go out as martyrs for a righteous cause. To them, the absolute control of manipulating everyone's beliefs was wrong. They believe it was no different then the Romans persecuting the Christians.

At the end of the speech was a statement that stated they acted alone. There are many other rebels but none of them ordered the attack. Then he gives a shout out to all rebel groups and leaders. Especially the leader known as Megan.

"Thank you," President Templeton states.

"Now what," Jarius asks.

There's a moment of silence and President Templeton ends it. "We go on as planned."

"But the memorial is a mess," I respond.

"I know. Trust me, it'll work."

After the meeting, Jarius talks with us for a while. He then lets us have the remaining part of the day off so we can rest.

AJ and I meet at a downtown Mexican restaurant. We clean up so it doesn't look like we came from a construction site. After we order our meals, AJ breaks the silence.

"What do you think of the 'One Nation Under God' speech continuing as usual?"

"It shows a very powerful image," I respond. "That nothing will stop this president. Nothing."

"And..." AJ says but trails off. I know this trick.

"And what?"

"It also gives him what he needs."

"What are you talking about," I ask. Sometimes AJ can be a little strange or mysterious.

"Remember we said that he wants to unify the nation."

"Right."

"Nether of us thinks it can happen with just a speech."

"Right, so..." I was about to ask but it comes to me. "After an attack, his speech will unify the country even more."

"Exactly. The rebels might have accidentally done the opposite of what they wanted."

"So now what," I ask, not really expecting an answer.

"I hope you studied your Bible," AJ responds. "At least according to the government."

"I hope you're joking. I really do."

Part 4

I was hoping AJ was wrong about a government takeover on religion, but it happened. It was about a little more than eleven months ago that the Lincoln Memorial was bombed. President Templeton gave a marvelous speech on a unified nation. He implored the people that his plan was two-fold. One part was to God and the other for people. He convinced the people that God working through the citizens of America has designed the administration to formulate the unity plan.

Except for the rebels, more people agreed with President Templeton in the nation as being one. There where many people in the middle on President Templeton's plan but more were switching. People from all political backgrounds, ethnic groups, gender, and of course, religious denominations began to agree. The top Christian leaders where used to promote the new belief to all people. To the President, if we have one denomination then we can truly be unified and represent that to the world.

Over the past year, the Lincoln Memorial was being renovated for Independence Day. The plan was to reveal a new America that will have the same ideals and mindset. President Templeton wanted to make sure that where destruction happened by a few, great things will come about to many.

An image is being considered as a means to symbolize the new direction. First it was just an idea; a throw away line by Jessica that will help people to remember. From there it grew and the idea became an actual thing.

The image was not something to worship as many rebels pronounced. Instead, it was a symbol of how we are one nation uniformed with a similar belief and purpose. Similar to how the flag represents a political force for a country or state. Football helmets have a symbol of the organization or college they represent. Even companies have a brand or logo to symbolize them. This is what the image was supposed to be.

There was much discussion on what it should be. Many staffers stated the traditional symbols of Christianity. Symbols like Jesus profile, the cross, a lamb, dove, and even a crown of thorns. President Templeton didn't want this because it might look like blasphemy. Many of the ministers he consulted were not in favor of those types symbols. They didn't want the country to look like it was in fact the new God.

It wasn't until early winter that the President demanded an idea. Jarius got the office workers together to brainstorm. The image was very important and had to be completed by Independence Day. I didn't think it was necessary and was weary of a created image. President Templeton desired an image because the idea of one denomination was taking hold across the nation.

Ministers from various denominations began preaching to people the new standard in reading the Bible. At first, many people were weary of this new teaching. The government used propaganda and flowery words from various religious leaders that changed their minds. The government did not have to push hard because many people wanted to be unified.

The ministers used Biblical evidence and historical facts to back up their sermons. The amazing thing was how easy the vast majority went along. AJ pointed out to me that it was easy to change because the government helped various churches and charities financially who pushed their agenda. With a heavy influence of cash, pastors didn't have to speak about blessing and money but concentrate on the new doctrine of the unified religion.

People around the world liked the ideas so much that many of them started to change. We are a nation who sends missionary workers to the world and they preached whatever their home churches taught. People where converting to the new denomination and the President really wanted a symbol.

At the meeting, we turned in our ideas. AJ told me his was the clouds with a lightening bolt; he wanted to show something about America's power coming from the Heavens. It's an interesting concept but probably not a winner. AJ knew that and desired to fail. He did not want to be a part of a false image. What if people started worshipping the image was his fear. He would have accidentally designed a new god for the world to worship. That was something he did not want on his conscious while burning in hell. I agree with him.

There where ideas that range from a beast similar to the Kraken in 'Wrath of the Titans' and the beasts of Daniel. Some said a tree. A few suggested various horses and other land animals. Others mentioned letters in specialized fonts and italics. My idea was an Eagle because it's already the symbol of America.

I won.

Jarius loved the idea and so did everyone else. Including President Templeton. I was joking about the Eagle but it caught on. They realized that using the symbol that we already use was perfect. It was something America is comfortable with because we have a connection to that animal. It's still illegal to kill or hunt Bald Eagles and it doesn't replace traditional Christian symbols. Instead, it served as a reminder of our government's standardizing religion.

The idea of the image was received and Golden Bald Eagles began to show up everywhere. Some had side views others the full bust. Most images were gold but some people got bronze due to cost restrictions. Golden Bald Eagles started showing up everywhere as statues and on posters as well.

Many of the posters had the golden image with the date of July 4th and 'New America' underneath. I could not believe that one decision, a stupid one by me, is everywhere. AJ would joke that I had better enjoy ice water because it will be scarce where I'm going.

Its a few week before the new America begins and the unveiling of a giant Golden Bald Eagle will be revealed. I'm at home in Sheridan Falls just to relax and rest the mind. Its weeks before the laws of squashing the rebellion will be enacted. The government will not tolerate rebels. Instead, the courts will brand them as traitors to the country.

The decision to label rebels as traitors was controversial. Some Americans thought it was good for the nation. Many people believe otherwise. Others left for Canada in fear of what would happen. They didn't want to be persecuted for having a different mindset or belief. A person could be punished by death if they are found to be a rebel. Being a rebel under the new laws meant a traitor and terrorist to the nation.

Death. Forget the true due process of a normal trial. It was death. Some assumed it was a joke but I know the people who were building death penalty chambers. These 'chambers' was like a huge furnace. The device is supposed to scare people so no one would rebel. The government uses the furnace, propaganda, and various other sources to crush the rebel movement. Some groups hung around and talked about a leader known as Megan.

I see graffiti throughout the city with Megan's name on them. Some signs had freedom, choice, and rebels on them. Many of these signs were in Washington D.C. as well as Sheridan Falls. One sign near my parents home had 'We will not go away', and Megan's name underneath.

I knock on my parents' door. Mom greets me with a smile and hug. They invite me in and offer some tea. Mom loves tea.

"How is everything," Mom asks.

"Good," I respond.

"See Teresa, all this stuff is getting to him," dad says. Mom waves him off and pays attention to me.

"How's work?"

"Well," I start and look around the house. A small golden bald eagle head was sitting on the fireplace. "You got one too," I ask.

"You know Jason," dad responds. "He's very convincing plus everyone has one. I heard they're building a large version of this thing in D.C."

He is right. A huge 90 foot-tall golden Bald Eagle is nearing completion and will have a home near Memorial park. It will be close to the Lincoln memorial with room for a store. Lights will shine upon it and there will be plenty of space for people to gather around. I thought the poster and small eagles was a bit much to promote the new image and religion of America. Having a 90-foot tall statue was crazy. I cannot believe my random suggestion turned to something like this. I should have chosen an iguana or octopus. At least it would have been rejected.

"Yeah."

"Not happy," dad asks.

"Felix," mom starts, "You shouldn't push him."

"Its okay, he's right. Seems funny you know."

"It's the new thing," mom says. "Everyone is doing it and just think all the denominations are actually peaceful with one another. Even non-Christians."

"Yeah but it still seems strange," dad says. "But you have to feel good son."

"Why?"

"Jason said they used your idea for the eagle to represent the nation as a symbol of unity."

"I was surprised."

"Still because of you, many will now have a new symbol to honor America. Kind of," mom says.

I can't believe it's my fault. Not really. I didn't come with the idea of an image to represent the new belief system. Jessica did that.

My concept for the Eagle is no different then the staff Moses used to heal people from venomous snakes. Eventually the staff became an idol that the people worshiped and had to be destroyed. I have a feeling that soon, so will this image or statue. This eagle is suppose to stand for something political but can become a thing of worship.

My parents want me to stay but I have to go and think. Coming home was good because it allows me to come back to my roots. Now I can think about what is right. Should I go with the majority or become a secret rebel. I don't want to die, but this new belief does not sit right with me.

After seeing my parents I go to Victory Temple and speak with Pastor Tyrone. A few golden eagles greet me in the driveway as I pull in. Inside are a few smaller golden eagles and posters about the ceremony on Independence Day. He's alone in his office and happy to see me. I wasn't sure if he would be in but assumed he was here. Pastor Tyrone loves doing his study at church. He always recognizes that it's a job and he takes it seriously.

"Good to see you," Pastor Tyrone says. His smile is large and full of bright teeth.

"You as well," I respond. "How's everything?"

"It's going," he says. His response is tight. Pastor knows my position.

"Its okay," I start, "you can be honest."

"I am," he says then sighs. "It's just that I'm torn."

"Torn?"

"Yeah, I'm thrilled at church attendance. It's always full. Some weekends we have three services."

"Three, impressive."

"Yeah but, are they here because they want to be? Do they love the Lord? Or are they're just scared?"

I nod. "Fear won't get you into Heaven," I respond.

"Not at all Sherwood. Plus I'm limited on what I can preach."

"Limited?"

"Not limited, but I have to teach within the guidelines prescribed by the council."

The council was the ministers chosen by President Templeton who represented the various Christian denominations. They decided and prescribed the doctrine. Pastor Tyrone had some room to be creative but had to stay within the doctrinal boundaries.

"Do you think God approves," I ask.

"Not sure," he says. "It seems great. We're all one."

"But something gnawing at you isn't it. Like something is wrong," I respond.

"Yes," Pastor Tyrone says without hesitation. "God can force us at anytime. He doesn't need your Uncle to help Him."

"I see."

Pastor Tyrone looks at his desk and then at the water container. "Where's my manners, want something to drink?"

"I'm fine and don't worry. I won't say a word." He smiles.

I leave Victory Praise and a few minutes later, pulled over by a police officer. I didn't see a stop sign and feel stupid. First day back in a few months and already, I'm in trouble. A police officer I partially recognize walks up to the window and studies my face. He pauses and smiles.

"Are you Felix Sheridan's kid," the officer asks.

"Yes sir," I respond.

"Sherwood right," he asks.

"Yes sir."

He reaches inside the car to shake my hand. "Please to meet you," he says.

"Thanks officer," I respond.

"I heard you came up with the image of the golden eagle."

"Yeah but…"

"I think that's fantastic," the officer states. "I'm officer Pace Brown."

"Nice to meet you, sorry for running the stop sign," I apologize.

"Not a problem. I know you have important things to do, working for the President."

"True."

"He's great," Pace says. "Getting the country together on one accord. It's what this country needs. Some moral values."

"So you approve," I ask.

"Do I? Yes sir I do. I wish I could go to the dedication of the Eagle."

"It doesn't' bother you that it's not a Christian symbol or a cross or something."

"Not at all," Pace responds. "To me it's great to bring God into our country. It's what we need. If only you knew about some of the mistakes I made when I was young." He sighs. "That was an awful summer, felt out of control. Much like this country, but now, thanks to Jesus, I'm whole. Like this country will be."

"Glad you approve," I lie.

"Watch out though. Some residents around here are a little shaky."

"Rebels," I ask.

"No, well, I hope not. Even though I do have my eye on someone."

"Really?"

"Yeap," Pace responds. He looks around and gets close to me through the window. "I don't want to get anyone in trouble."

"You won't."

"But I know a guy name Carlisle; he's always been one to fight authority and bullies."

"Interesting," I say.

"We've been friends since high school but he doesn't agree with the new laws."

I say, "You haven't arrested him?"

Pace laughs. "Can't do that, not a law. Yet. But that will all change after Independence Day."

"True," I respond. "Do you know where I can find him?"

Pace looks at me with surprise. He's still good friends with Carlisle and don't want to hurt him. He knows my position and family. I'm sure it will not take long before he realizes the President is my uncle.

"Not to cause trouble," I respond, "just to talk. Maybe I can change his mind. Bring your friend back."

"Of course," Pace responds. "He owns a theater on First Street. There all the time."

"Thanks Officer."

After talking with Officer Brown, I make my way to the theater. I'm sure Carlisle will try to contact me. I remember a story from dad about him. I believe he stood up to some bullies at Wedgewood. It makes sense that he would view America and the government as a bully. It's a chance but I hope Carlisle knows about the underground resistance. Especially Megan.

After paying for a movie and getting some popcorn with soda, I make my way to the film. It didn't matter what I was watching. I'm hoping that Carlisle is here and sees me.

The trailers end and my film is about to start. A tap on my shoulder causes me to look around. A guy, who looks close to my dad's age, sits behind me. He has an intense look on his face and no smile.

"I know you being here isn't by accident," the man says.

"No," I respond. "Its not."

"We have to talk."

"When," I ask.

"Now," he says and slips me a piece of paper. I follow the instructions and get up ten minutes later. Finally, I can find out more about the resistance and the rebels. I hope Carlisle is someone who can lead me to Megan.

Part 5

I meet Carlisle in a small eatery called Ocean's Café. It looks new and is close to the theater. Carlisle is a stocky man who has a touch of gray down the side of his head. His glasses are thin and rest on the edge of his nose. His face has a constant frown as though life has been hard for him to protect others.

Carlisle is sitting in the back of the café and I sit across from him after getting a doughnut. He has a dark coffee but it hasn't been touch. He clearly did not come here for food.

"So," I begin but he puts a hand up.

"I know who you are," Carlisle states.

"Okay."

"And I have a feeling I know what you're searching for."

"You mean who," I respond.

"I mean what," Carlisle says. "A concept, an idea, like your, idol." He pauses a little before saying idol and sits back with a grin.

"Not mine."

"Maybe, maybe not, but I digress." I look around the place. No one is paying us any attention. There are no cameras or people trying to record me with this guy. None of them will go and rat me out to Jarius, a loyalist, or the President. "Like I said, you're looking for a concept."

"Let's say that I am," I respond.

"What you have to understand, Sherwood," Carlisle says and emphasis my name in the sentence. "Having the ability to defend the weak and powerless is a good thing. It's a great idea that can sometimes make the person a bully if it's not held in check. Sometimes we do things forcibly to people because we think it's the right thing. Even if it's against their will."

That's deep and I allow what he says to wash over my mind. I understand the message but want to know something else. "I'm curious, how do you know anything about me," I ask.

"Your last name is the same as the city," Carlisle responds. "This town isn't that big, so it's easy to keep track of those who have been here all their lives. And others who are making a big splash on a national level."

"You went to school with President Templeton," I ask.

"No, he attended Brent," Carlisle responds. "They had their own issues over there, but that didn't stop until Takashi stepped up. Now there's a great hero."

"I see."

"But what do you want to know about the rebellion," Carlisle asks quietly but not soft as a whisper. He of course couldn't let random people know about the rebellion or that he knew about them. I look around the room. No one moved when he asked about the rebellion. We could be amongst friends. I wouldn't be surprise if most of the customers in here were supportive of the rebels cause.

"Who is Megan," I ask.

"A concept," Carlisle laughs out. "It's a concept. No different then your golden image that your office came up with."

I look around Ocean's Café and study the walls. No golden eagles. The movie theater was the same way. I'm right about this place being sympathetic to the rebellion. This makes me in prime enemy territory due to my job. The name of the place is familiar. I believe an ex-basketball player was named Ocean. That's why it is throwing me off. At first, I assume it's a fish restaurant when I entered but Ocean is the name of the owner.

"That was an accident."

"So it's true, you came up with that thing?"

"No not the entire concept of an image. A different person did that but the Eagle was my idea. That was a mistake."

"Mistake?"

"Yeap, I didn't think they would take that seriously. It's an image of a bird, I'm scared."

"Scared," Carlisle asks.

"Yeah, what if they start worshiping it?"

"Start," he laughs. "They already have."

Clearly, I'm confused and Carlisle can see it. He chuckles and shakes his head. He takes a sip of his dark coffee and frowns. I thought he wasn't a fan of the drink.

"People already have a name for it."

"It?"

"The golden image. The Eagle. The new god."

"No I didn't name it," I responded. "It's a symbol of our unity. It is not a god or something to be worshipped. Like the golden calf or Dagon."

Carlisle laughs and hits the table. "You said that like a teleprompter was over my shoulder."

"I know it's crazy, but it's true."

"Isaiah," he responds.

"Who's Isaiah?"

"The image you, I mean, the image that is ready to be revealed," Carlisle says. "Others call it J.C. and even some Archalus, which is just strange."

"Isaiah," I whisper. "Why that?" Before Carlisle responds, I put my hand up. I get it.

One of the scriptures to help with spreading the message of the image was Isaiah 40:31. The quote is, 'But they that wait upon the Lord shall renew their strength. They shall mount up with wings as an eagle. They shall run and not be weary, and they shall walk and not faint.' Of course, we chose that scripture to reveal a power within the country that will not falter. Having the message stem from the Bible makes the administration's laws ordained by God.

"Oh wow," I respond.

"I'm not sure of you, and your mission, but someone wants to meet you," Carlisle states

"Who?"

"Megan."

"I thought you said Megan is a concept."

"It is," Carlisle responds. "You'll see. It's real, or should I say they're real, but it's the concept behind it."

I can't believe Megan wants to meet me. Strange. Especially with my position on the Presidential cabinet. It's not as if everyone knows but clearly, the rebellion keeps up.

"Okay," I respond. "When and where?"

A few days after talking with Carlisle I head back to D.C. Of course, while in Sheridan Falls I saw my parents again. It was great talking with some of my friends and seeing the beach and falls. After that, it was on to the Nation's Capital to meet Megan.

Carlisle was specific about where to meet the rebellion's leader. The direction was for me to park at a specific spot and they would take me to Megan. The site is in an empty parking lot in Herndon, Virginia. I sit for a while when two guys show up in a SUV. I get in the back seat and they cover my head. Not a surprise. I figure that would happen and go along with the ride.

After what feels like thirty minutes or more we arrive at our destination. I haven't heard too many planes above so we're probably away from both major airports. Herndon is close to Dulles so that would mean we are even further into Virginia. No matter I'm not worried.

The meeting place is a home and we go downstairs to a finished basement. At least twenty people are already there. Various ages but most are young like teenagers. One person is probably still in middle school.

They all stare. It's a little unnerving. I'm sure they all know who I am but I have no idea about them. The new religious laws are going to happen in a few days and here I am with a local group of rebels. Strange. Especially since after July 4th, all rebels will be arrested for treason.

"Sit," a voice says from behind.

I didn't notice the chair behind me and sit down. A tall man, probably the voice I heard, comes from behind me and walks to the front. He is the oldest person in the room. I wonder more if he was Megan. Maybe that's what Carlisle meant. That Megan was a concept to throw people, like Jarius and myself, off from finding their true leader.

"You Megan," I ask. The room erupts in laughter. That idea was wrong. There must be a real woman named Megan.

"No," he responds, "I'm Crawford, she's Megan."

A woman walks from behind me. I can smell her scent and it's familiar. I know that scent. My eyes perk up once I see who it is.

"Jessica," I say when she stands in front of me.

"Megan," she responds. "At least while I'm here."

"You're the rebel leader," I ask.

"How do you think we knew so much," Crawford says.

"Where you behind the Lincoln attack?"

"No," Jessica responds. "They where on their own."

"You came up with the idea of the image," I say.

"And you came up with his form," she responds.

There was silence and then we both laugh. "Amazing what the two of us have done."

"Exactly," she says.

"Jarius said he thought someone was a rebel on the staff. He would be incensed if he knew it was you."

Jessica raises an eyebrow and smiles. "Yeah, true."

That's what Carlisle meant by a symbol. Megan wasn't the real leader name but a fake one. She was a symbol for the rebellion to live on in spite of any opposition. This was similar to the golden image representing worship and belief according to the government; Megan is the symbol of free worship.

"What do you want with me," I ask.

"How do you feel about the new laws, the administration? I remember how you felt during the paintball game several years ago."

"True."

"Back then you was serious about standing up for what you believe. What are you willing to do now?"

I pause for a moment. Look around the room. A pit was growing in my stomach. There was a feeling that felt good but bad. Nervousness. What is Jessica willing to give up for her convictions? The rebellion created a fake name for the leader so that way the message would continue. This meant even if the real leader dies the ideal will live on forever.

"What do you have in mind?"

Independence Day. The nation is thrilled with the new laws. President Templeton will have the signing broadcast from the oval office so the nation and world can be a part. To him it's a great day for all people and an awesome day for God.

Various golden images are all over the place. T-shirts, posters, banners, and even little statues and souvenirs have the "Isaiah's" or golden eagles on them. Even churches have golden eagles in their sanctuary while office buildings have theirs in the lobby.

President Templeton signs the law with his son Jarius on the right and the golden eagle to his left. The Vice-President is near the side with various other leaders from both the Senate and House. There are cheers in the oval office as well throughout the country when the signature is complete. The law that so many campaigned and promoted is finally in effect. Everyone, living in America will have to follow the new state run religion or imprisoned for treason.

The celebration moves from the oval office to the newly reconstructed Lincoln Memorial. To the side of the building is a large statue covered with a sheet. Everyone knows what its underneath but wait with anticipation for the unveiling.

It is a bright summer day so I can only imagine how great and full of splendor the image will look. A large choir and marching band surrounds the front of the statue. On cue, they play hymns of some sort with the band playing the music. The song was churchy and part patriotic at the same time, if that makes sense?

Many people wait in church while the law is signed watching the events on television. There is an immense crowd around the image and in Memorial Park. Many residents couldn't make it downtown so they stay at home or went to their respective places of worship. President Templeton stated a few days ago that all people would share a special prayer during the ceremony. He believed that God wants a nation praying together for the future.

AJ, Jessica, and I are in the office. Most of the staff gathers around the large flat screen in the lobby. Some went to churches but we thought it would be great to be here together. There are various images of the golden eagle in the office. None is in my office but someone put a poster on the back of my door. I have no plans to keep that and will remove it later.

I already know what President Templeton's speech will contain. He will talk about the importance of being a unified nation. Comparison will be made to Lincoln himself as both worked to bring the country together. During Lincoln's time, it was for freedom, economic, and political reasons. Currently it is for moral and spiritual awakening. President Templeton desired the symbol of Lincoln as a background to show the nation that a few violent rebels will not tear this country apart. That's the same message Jessica had for Crawford.

Crawford wanted to do what the original guys did a while back. He didn't want to blow himself up, but maybe kill or shoot some leaders who are a part of the bill. Crawford realizes he could die but did not mind going down in a blaze of glory. He was all about a violent confrontation. Jessica reminded him that the last group only brought the nation closer to the government's plan. Instead, she wanted to use other means to get the rebels message. Crawford was calm and agreed with her.

Most of our co-workers are excited over the big reveal. Jarius is near his dad as President Templeton walks up to the podium. The cheers were deafening. I think I can hear them from the office, but doubt it. Thousands possibly a million crowd Memorial park and watch the televisions that are set up throughout the park. Some even gather in the various Smithsonian museums to watch the broadcast.

After much fan fair, Isaiah, the eagle, is reveal with the choir singing and the band playing. Just as I thought, the sun glistens off the ninety-foot tall statue of the eagle. I'm sure in person it made some people squint because on plasma screen it's bright.

The actual image sat on a thirty-foot tall platform so the Eagle was actually 60 feet tall. I'm sure to most it's huge and bright because of the coating of gold. The image was completed faster then normal with many artisans working on it non-stop. They didn't have a design until I opened my mouth. I still can't believe I suggested an Eagle.

"Let us pray as one," President Templeton says.

People around me bow their heads while others prostrate themselves towards the television screen. I'm sure people in churches, business, home, and everywhere else did the same. I assume most did the same across the land building a powerful praying front.

I'm sure there are others like Jessica, AJ, and myself who decide not to bow down before the new image. We stand and keep our heads high and eyes wide open. In reality, we could have bowed and prayed to God as normal. However, in this case, we didn't want the look of praying to a false image.

"Hey guys," one of the co-workers say, "you need to kneel or at least bow your head."

I look in their direction. It came to me that I could respond but instead shake my head. The three of us stand and I fold my arms in open defense, and AJ does the same.

An officer in the room looks in our direction and motions for us to bow down. Already the President has begun a prayer but we refuse.

"Hey, get down," the officer states.

I ignore him and turn my back to the television. My Uncle won't even get the satisfaction with that image being shown simultaneously. Even though he doesn't know that. After the prayer, the officer comes to me and stands in my face.

"Did you hear what I said," the man shouts. His breath was in need of a mint. He was close. To close, but that doesn't matter.

"Yes," I respond.

"Why didn't you bow down and pray," he asks.

"I do not worship false images or a fake god."

The officer punches me in the stomach, which is unexpected. I double over and fall to my knees. That's one way of forcing somebody to kneel. Still I will not pray, especially since I can barely breathe.

"That's uncalled for," Jessica yells and runs over. The officer pulls out his gun and points it at her. Our co-workers ignore the speech after the prayer and pay attention to what's happening in the room.

"I have trouble," the officer states into a radio. "Possible rebellious faction in the office." Then an okay on the other side and he keeps the gun on all three of us. "Over there." The officer points in a particular direction and we fall in line. My stomach still hurts but I make my way to the wall. Some of our coworkers are on their phones. They text and put information onto their network pages about what is happening.

A few more officers come into the room and lead us to a holding cell within the white house. They lock us together in a cell and have three officers standing by the door. Two officers are on either side of the cell's outer door but we sit and rest.

Time passes and we hear a door open down the hall. The footsteps are fast and in a hurry. The person is clearly upset. Finally, we see who it is.

"Sherwood, Jessica, and Aaron," Jarius says. "What have you done?"

Part 7

"Please tell me there has been a mistake," Jarius asks.

I'm sure the ceremony is still going on and he had no plans to miss it. After the speech, there are some more singing, liturgical dancing, and a few other celebration events. Even some fireworks and fighter jets fly-over is planned.

"No mistake," AJ responds.

Jarius is in the cell with us pulsating with anger. Clearly, he's enraged. "Then it is true that when prayer went out, you three decided to go against it."

"Yes," we say in unison. We even look at each other and grin.

"You think this is funny? You think this is a game?" We shake our heads. "Some of our coworkers put you on the web and other sites to talk about your behavior and betrayal."

"We couldn't help that," Jessica responds.

"Yes you could. It was simple. Bow down then pray," Jarius says.

"That went against what we believe," I say.

"What you believe," Jarius states. He's so angry it's as if the words slither out his mouth. "Jessica you came up with the idea of an image, and Sherwood you thought of it as an eagle. The both of you formulated the image."

"I didn't think you would be serious," Jessica says. "I thought of something for people to worship Christ. Not this thing you created as a false god."

"False god," Jarius yells. "That is not a false god. We worship Jesus Christ you idiot. That eagle is the country's representation to God that we recognize His authority in our lives and government. That's it."

"That eagle, which is now named, Isaiah, is an image that represents your leadership, not Jesus Christ," I shout.

"I cannot believe you two. I figure Aaron would be the traitor."

"Hey," AJ says.

"But you two," Jarius begins. He walks around and then returns his gaze on me. "We're family Sherwood and I'm ..."

"Dating the enemy," Jessica finishes for Jarius.

"To put it mildly," Jarius says. "I'm ashamed."

There's a slight pause and no word is spoken. Jarius looks down at the floor then at us. "Who is Megan and where can we find her?"

"What makes you think we know that," AJ asks.

"All you rebels know about that. The three of you being so high up in this cabinet should know something," Jarius responds. There's a pause and nod at one another. "Where is she," he yells

"Right here," Jessica responds.

"In this office," Jarius asks.

"In this cell. I'm Megan. Or at least the assume leader of the rebellion in this area, known as Megan," Jessica responds.

"You ordered the Lincoln attack," Jarius ask. Funny I thought the same thing. Neither of us paid attention to the guy clearly stating that no other rebel group had anything to do with that attack.

"No, we had nothing to do with that."

"To get people to no longer listen to one image that was set up with God's help, you decide to create something else to worship," Jarius says.

"No, well, no," Jessica answers. "We gave people an opportunity to choose. Like how it was before. Instead of leadership or the government telling them who to worship."

"It's perfect," Jarius says.

"What's perfect," I ask.

"The plan. For a long time we've gathered various Christian ministers, pastor, bishops, scholars, and lay people to create the perfect Christian religion."

Jarius goes into details on how each religion or denomination wasn't perfect on their own. Instead, they emphasized a piece of the higher truth.

The group his father gathered decided to combine central aspect of each denomination with God's help. A few of the ideas that came out where, baptism by immersion plus emphasis on the Spirit and speaking in various tongues. The church will be more charismatic and exciting to draw all people around the world. They even decided to keep a particular day holy and close down business and sporting events to make sure it was special. A hierarchy was developed according to some denominations to keep the group organized and control. In the future an over all clergy leader will be chosen to head the new religion. Even complicated truths in Daniel and Revelations were explained plus the state of the dead and many other dividing truths where meshed together. After Jarius said his spill, he feels convinced that his point was proven. It's clean in his mind that what the administration have done is special. To Jarius, God ordained the plan.

"You expect us to believe this new religion just because a group of guys got together," AJ states.

"Let me remind you Aaron," Jarius starts and glares at AJ. His eyes squint from anger. "That it was at various conferences that groups of men who got together to canonize The Bible as we now know it."

AJ looks at me and I nod. It's true. "Oh," AJ responds.

"Did you assume that the Bible just amazingly came together? At one point it was in various books and many people had disagreements on which book should be allowed in the Bible. Even today, various Christian groups have different forms of the Bible. Until now."

AJ is stunned but I can tell that he's still defiant. Learning of this new truth is surprising but doesn't change his mind.

"Those guys where not trying to change something. The Lord ultimately used them to put together a book that will help people build a relationship with Him," Aaron says.

Jarius sighs. He stops looking at AJ and then at me. "Now that I have spoken will you agree to bow down when the call is given and pray?"

"No," I respond. AJ and Jessica agree.

"Then you will be sorry," another voice says from beyond the cell. We all look up to see President Templeton. Secret service members surround him. He's even angrier then Jarius.

"Uncle, how nice to see you," I say.

"You have three days to think about your decision," President Templeton responds completely ignoring my greeting. "After that if you do not worship what we have set up you will be held for treason and burn in the correction chamber."

Three days came and went. We are given Bibles and government standard religious material to study. During the time, we read the Bible even more but not according to their guidelines. It was refreshing getting the word of God by how He interprets. That was much better compare to what the government mandates. Even though all of their truths weren't wrong. Still you can tell that it is slanted towards loving the nation more then self. I know where this will lead. Eventually it will be loving the nation more then God.

Their new image and religion is about control. President Templeton and Jarius with many others want control over the citizens. The easiest way to do that was through religion and belief.

So many people have great ideas. They desire to do something for the Lord and then muck it up with their actions. To unify the country is great. To force people to believe a certain way is not.

We didn't change our minds and is more defiant. After three days they guide us from our cell and then to the room with the large furnace. It's called the trial room or correction chamber. This was nothing like a true trial room because a large furnace like object is at the back and rows of chairs on the other side. This feels more like the execution room. I heard about the furnace but thought it was a metaphor for being imprisoned for treason. Not literally, be burned like the three men in Babylon.

"Greetings fellow Americans," Templeton starts. "We have clearly stated that all those who do not follow our new state religion will be looked upon as traitors to the country. After all we have sat down and formulated the perfect belief system to have on Earth and make it into Heaven."

Cheers roar through the auditorium. Jarius cheers from his seat near the front and to the side. Various leaders fill the room with a few lay people throughout. The three of us sit in dull grey outfits with hands tied behind our back.

"In my own cabinet, my own team, close to me, is traitors to God and this land." Boos fill the room. "But we are merciful and kind."

President looks at us. To our side is a replica of the golden eagle that is near us. "All I ask is that you pray in the direction of the new image as a symbol that you agree with our rules, laws, and doctrines ordained by God."

"No," we respond.

"No," President Templeton says. "You were chosen as a part of my staff, you dated my son, and you're flesh and blood," he says while pointing at AJ, Jessica, and me. "How do you turn down God's will?"

"It's not God. It's you," I respond. "This is your will, your control. It has nothing to do with God."

"Blasphemy will not be tolerated," Templeton states. "If you will not pray then I will have no choice but to denounce you as traitors to the land and cleanse you in the fiery furnace."

"Then we will be cleansed," Jessica says.

"Who is your god that is able to save you from my hands," president Templeton states.

"I'm not going to debate you Uncle," I say. "But you have created a false idol and have used it as a means of control. Our only mission as believing Christians is to inform people of the world of Jesus Christ and His message of love and soon return. True connection comes from Him, not your laws. Not in your hands."

"We have a personal relationship with God. Not because of mandate but because we love Him," Jessica says. AJ nods in agreement.

"So you defy the country," President Templeton says.

"We decide to stand up to a higher authority. God's. Not this false image you have created," AJ states. He nods his head in the direction of the golden eagle.

"And the true God we serve is more then able to save us from your hands, but if not, then let it be known that we will not serve your image or any other false idol you create. There are others like us who believe in the true savior Jesus Christ," I say.

"To the furnace," Templeton orders.

The large furnace is on. The heat rages and they raise the temperature even more. The crowd is amazed at its powerful glow and can feel the warmth of its heat. A few of the guards grab a hold of us and throw us in from the front. The heat alone kills them but we land in the midst of the furnace.

The roar of the fire is deafening as it is all around us. We look at one another and to our amazement; none of us are in pain. I thought it was fake until I see the guards lying on the ground and burning. President Templeton looks in. He clearly sees something with us in the furnace and is pale. It looks like he says something but the fire is too loud. The roar continues and we see him point to the side. The next thing we know the fire is off.

"Come out," President Templeton orders.

We climb out of the furnace and walk towards him. The ropes that were binding us are gone. Our bodies and clothes are perfect. The crowd is amazed, especially Jarius. He's the only one that doesn't look hurt or sorry for what just happen.

President Templeton falls to his knees and begins to cry some. "I'm so sorry," he says. "I just wanted to help unify the country."

I reach my hand down and pull him up. We hug each other while one person from the crowd runs to the golden eagle and throw it against the wall. I can tell Jarius wants to say something but chooses not to. He stares at us for a while and walks out the room while others come in our direction.

President Templeton agrees to take down the large golden eagle by the Lincoln memorial. No longer will he force people to worship a certain way. God has spoken to him and he is now listening. Uncle Jason has to figure out a different way to unify the country without forcing people to believe a certain way. The President vetoes the plan to force religion on people but Jarius is not thrilled. We know there are many who believe in Jarius' plan and now they are the new rebels of the golden image. The nation can't worry about him but move on from Jarius' perfect plan and go according to the will of a perfect God.

Be strong and stand up for God's standard not society.